The Wrong Omega
BANGERS & MASH

MM FARMER

THE WRONG OMEGA

Copyright ©2022 by Merry Farmer

This ebook is licensed for your personal enjoyment only. This ebook may not be re-sold or given away to other people. If you would like to share this book with another person, please purchase an additional copy for each recipient. If you're reading this book and did not purchase it, or it was not purchased for your use only, then please return to your digital retailer and purchase your own copy. Thank you for respecting the hard work of this author.

This book is a work of fiction. Names, characters, places, and incidents are products of the author's imagination or are used fictitiously. Any resemblance to actual events or locales or persons, living or dead, is entirely coincidental.

Cover design by Erin Dameron-Hill (who is completely fabulous)

ASIN: B0B7879WK1

Paperback: 9798843896003

Click here for a complete list of other works by Merry Farmer.

If you'd like to be the first to learn about when the next books in the series come out and more, please sign up for my newsletter here: http://eepurl.com/RQ-KX

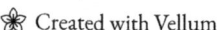 Created with Vellum

Ty

I was the best Emergency Support Alpha in the business. Thinking that wasn't any sort of arrogance on my part, it was a fact. I had been with Bangers & Mash for nearly ten years, since graduating from Barrington University with a degree in psychology *summa cum laude* and being recruited directly to work for B&M by Salazar Banger himself. I'd worked my way up from trainee ESA to Assistant Director in just five years, and in the last five, I'd not only helped teach training classes for new alphas to the program, I'd also begun helping with plans to expand the business into other cities by setting up B&M branches along the East Coast.

Which was why, even though I was on my way to meet a client, I answered when Sal Banger's name popped up on the dashboard screen of my Ranger as I headed into Barrington.

"Morning, boss," I answered the call, keeping my eyes on

the road and my grip on the steering wheel tight. "Something wrong?"

"Morning, Ty. No, not at all," Sal said in the deep, alpha rumble his voice always had. It made people think he was angry when actually, Sal Banger was one of the nicest guys I had ever met. "You headed off the mountain before I had a chance to talk to you about the trip next week."

I winced slightly, frustrated with myself for setting out on this latest ESA call in such a hurry. "Sorry," I said. "Nick told me everything was taken care of for the trip and that I could head out. This omega sounded pretty eager to meet. He thinks his heat is going to start any second now."

"Is this the young guy? The one in his second year of medical school who can't be bothered to date?" Sal asked.

I was tempted to laugh at that characterization, but to do so would have been crass. It was none of my business why an omega hired an ESA to take them through their heat instead of turning to a partner or a trusted friend. Omegas almost always knew when heat was coming, and most of the ones I had ever known were either dating an alpha—or occasionally a strong beta—who could take them through, or they had an alpha friend who was willing to help them out.

Of course, the entire reason Sal Banger and Nick Mash had founded B&M was for those omegas who either didn't have anyone or who wanted just to get on with it and have the three or four disruptive days of their heat taken care of by a professional so they could avoid emotional attachment and get on with their lives.

That, and B&M had been founded so less fortunate omegas wouldn't be forced to sell their heat in the back alleys or underground networks of people who sought to take advantage of young men and women when they were at their most vulnerable.

"Yep," I answered Sal's question. "Doyle Curry. He said

his future career as a surgeon is everything to him, but he's worried about the stigma of heat in a profession that has traditionally been dominated by alphas and betas."

"Got it," Sal said. I could practically hear my boss nod on the other end of the call. "Well, good luck with him. You're meeting at The Grand, right?"

"Yep. Mr. Curry wanted a hotel instead of his residence, and the omega is always right."

Sal laughed. "Good. The Grand knows to charge the room to our account. I think Hamish is still there, recovering after his call the other day, so say hi if you see him."

"Will do," I said.

"Which brings me around to the purpose for my call," Sal went on, his tone shifting. "About this Norwalk trip next week."

"I'm looking forward to it," I said, cracking one of my rare smiles.

"Good," Sal said. "This expansion could be really good for us. Better still, it will be good for the omegas of Norwalk. Sanchez and Cross think so too."

Kevin Sanchez and his wife, Madeline Cross, were the financers who had pledged half the money needed to bring a B&M branch to Norwalk. The small industrial city was big enough to support a new B&M location, but didn't have the budget to fund it through tax dollars alone. Sanchez and Cross had stepped up to donate the cash needed to make the new branch a reality. I'd been working with them through email and video calls for a while now, and was scheduled to head to Norwalk in a week to iron out the last details and to get everyone to sign on the dotted line.

It was a huge step for Norwalk, and a big one for me personally as well. It was the first time Sal and Nick had trusted me with something as big as masterminding the opening of a new B&M branch, and it definitely represented a step up in my career.

And my career was everything to me. It wasn't just a job; it was a passion.

"I just had word from Sanchez and Cross," Sal went on as I turned my truck off the highway and headed along the city street that would take me closer to the beach, where The Grand was located. "They've offered to have you stay at their house as opposed to a hotel. Are you okay with that?"

"Yeah, sure," I said. I usually kept to myself when I was off the clock, especially if I was just coming off an ESA call, like I would be when I left for the trip. Omega hormones affected alphas too, even if I didn't have any deep emotional connection with my client. I usually took a few days off after calls, to unscramble my thoughts and return to equilibrium. But if the couple who wanted to donate that much money to build a branch wanted to entertain me for a few days personally, I wouldn't say no to it. I couldn't afford to with so much on the line.

"They sent around an itinerary as well," Sal said. "They've got you doing a tour of Norwalk which includes several sites they think would be good for an office, one of which is part of a special housing project they've spearheaded, and a meet-and-greet with the mayor and several town councilors. Does that work for you?"

"Anything you want, boss," I said. "You know my first and only priority is to B&M. I believe in the company, and I'm happy to see it expand."

"That's what I like to hear," Sal said, and I could hear a smile in his voice. "You're one of the best we've got, Ty. I don't know how we would manage without you."

I smiled again. Twice in one hour. It must have been a record. "Thanks, boss," I said. "And whatever it takes to get this new branch sorted, just let me know, and I'll do it."

"We'll have one last meeting in a few days, after your call," Sal said. "Until then, enjoy your call."

"Thanks, Sal."

I ended the call, feeling confident and looking forward to the trip next week. I shook my head a bit over the way Sal always told me to enjoy my ESA calls. I wasn't there to enjoy myself; I was there for the omega. Sure, taking an omega through heat was pleasurable. Heat sex was wildly good for both the alpha and the omega. Too many of my buddies liked to tease me about how lucky I was to be able to bang omegas in heat multiple times a month.

I didn't see it that way. I had a duty of care to the omegas who hired an ESA for their heat. They always had a sensitive reason why they wanted a professional for such an intimate encounter, and I had vowed ten years ago when I received my ESA license that I would always respect their reasons and their needs, particularly when they wanted to keep those reasons to themselves. It wasn't my place to question any omega, just to help them.

The Grand was located right along Barrington's busiest stretch of beach. It was centrally located in the seaside town, which meant the area and the hotel itself saw a lot of traffic, but the hotel was unfailingly discreet, and its owners were friends of Sal and Nick from way back. They'd struck up a deal to provide B&M with rooms for ESA calls at a discount, and they valued discretion as much as Sal and Nick did.

There were even a handful of parking spaces reserved for ESAs attending calls in the hotel's underground garage. I gratefully slid my Ranger into one of those places. I hated getting into a boiling hot truck after a call, when I was already overheated from days of absorbing omega hormones, and even though it wasn't the middle of summer yet, the sun was hot enough.

I got out, slung my overnight bag and the ESA heat kit I'd

picked up at B&M's mountain compound before leaving for the call over one shoulder, then locked my truck and started for the back entrance to the lobby, already running through not only the protocols for the call, but details of next week's trip as I walked.

I smelled the omega before I saw him. There was no scent on earth as delicious as an omega in heat. Ten years of going on multiple heat calls a month, and that first whiff of the client never got old.

This one was particularly strong, unusually so. The scent was like a lollipop. Not just any lollipop either. I was hit so hard with the memory of the gigantic lollipop my dad had bought for me on a family trip to the beach when I was eight—a lollipop that was bigger than my head and that I hadn't been able to make a dent in, let alone finish, even though I'd spent all day licking it—that I stopped for a second just to breath the scent in. My cock twitched hard, and if not for the tight restraint of my jeans, I would have instantly looked obscene.

But there was something else...off about the scent. Not to mention it was so strong that it was all around me and seeping into my pores, but I couldn't see another soul, let alone an omega, anywhere. An omega scent usually only got that strong after heat had already started. Sure, an omega's scent started to increase within a week of their heat starting, which was one way they knew it was coming, but it wasn't usually *that* strong until—

I spotted him as I stepped through the first of the lobby's two doors. The scent in the small, enclosed area between the two doors was so overpowering that I let out a low, alpha growl before I could stop myself. My dick filled so hard that, if I hadn't known better, I would have thought I was in danger of knotting without even being in an omega.

But that was all irrelevant the moment my gaze landed on

the small, lithe omega huddled into the fetal position in the corner of the vestibule, shaking like a leaf.

"Shit," I growled, moving faster as I approached the omega. I crouched beside the man, dropping my bag and kit, and reached out a hand to gently move the hood of the omega's hoodie back.

The man was young, definitely a college kid. He had thick, black hair that stuck out in every direction, which might have been the fault of the hood that he'd been hiding in. His skin was smooth and pale, like a lot of omegas, and he had the most gorgeous, full lips. I immediately envisioned them wrapped around my cock as I sank deep into the omega's throat.

I sucked in a breath and shook the fantasy away. It was a typical, hormonal reaction and not to be taken seriously. What did need to be taken seriously was the state the omega was in.

"Mr. Curry?" I asked.

The omega gave no response. He seemed to shake harder, now that I was close to him, and if I wasn't mistaken, the seat of the man's jeans was soaking wet.

There was no time for polite introductions. "I've got you, Mr. Curry," I said in the soothing voice I'd practiced for the last decade. "No need to worry. I'm here now, and we'll work through your heat together. It's going to be alright."

I reached over to hoist my bag and heat kit over my shoulder again, then scooped the omega into my arms. Omegas were naturally smaller and lighter than alphas and betas. I was able to lift Mr. Curry as if he weighed nothing.

Mr. Curry moaned as if the gesture caused him pain when I stood. It was likely the unique sort of pain omegas felt when they had gone for hours into their heat without any relief from an alpha, or even toys. The sensation had once been described to me as the sort of whole-body pain that was felt when someone had a kidney stone. I'd never had one, but that didn't mean I wouldn't take Mr. Curry's pain absolutely seriously and get him up to a room as quickly as possible.

"You're going to be alright, Mr. Curry," I repeated, carrying the omega into the hotel lobby. "I've got you now."

Mr. Curry groaned again, clutching at my shirt and burying his face into the crook of my neck. He drew in several long breaths of my alpha scent, which only made him moan more, then closed his mouth over the small bit of exposed skin at my collar, licking and sucking as though he could get what he needed that way.

It felt so damn good. My alpha instincts roared to life so hard that I nearly missed a step as I headed to the end of the lobby desk, where priority check-in was located.

"Looks like we have an emergency here," Raul, the daytime manager said before I made it all the way to the desk.

"And here I thought I would get to the hotel a little early to set things up before Mr. Curry was scheduled to arrive," I said, trying to keep my voice light for Mr. Curry's sake.

"No worries," Raul said. "Your room is already prepared. I've stocked it with a case of water and a few protein bars, even though I know you have them in that kit of yours." Raul held up his hand to fend off my protest before I could even make it.

He typed on the computer at the desk while he spoke, and took a plastic card from a pile and ran it through the scanner. "Room service knows you'll be here for the next three days, and they've been instructed to give you priority service, when you're ready. Housekeeping can come in discreetly whenever you want as well. We're all here to serve you, Mr. Martin."

"We're all here to serve the omega, you mean." I took the room card with an attempt at a smile for Raul, though my senses were short-circuiting because of how far into his heat Mr. Curry already was.

I wanted to shelter my omega, hide him against my body so no one could view my property. It was a typical alpha response, one I'd experienced plenty of times before and could usually ignore, but I'd never felt it this strong.

It had to be because Mr. Curry had misjudged the timing of his heat and let it go for too long before coming to the hotel. If he'd needed me to get there earlier, I would have. But that was water under the bridge now.

"Does Mr. Curry have any baggage to take up to the room?" Raul asked as I started to turn around.

I hadn't even thought about that, but from what I could see, there was none. It was unusual, but not unheard of. Some omegas brought very little with them on a call, as they spent most of the three days naked anyhow. And the hotel always provided robes and toiletries.

"I don't think so," I said, "but if we get settled and it turns out he left something in his car, I'll call down to you. I think he waited a bit too long before leaving for the hotel."

"Looks like it," Raul said with a sympathetic smile.

I felt bad for talking about Mr. Curry as if he wasn't there, but I could tell from the way the omega clutched at me and moaned plaintively with each breath that he was too far gone to care.

I nodded to Raul, then hurried off to the side, where the private elevator that took guests to the upper floors was located. I had to fumble a bit to use the card to activate the elevator and to give me clearance for the top floor, but once we were swooping upward, I began to feel easier.

"It's alright, Mr. Curry," I repeated my reassurances from downstairs. "We're on the way up to the room." I paused, and even though I wasn't one to make conversation with clients, I said, "Let me guess. You had a test of some sort you didn't want to miss, or you had rounds that you wanted to do before heading to the hotel. Is that why you're so far gone already?"

Mr. Curry didn't reply. As the elevator stopped, letting us out on the top floor, he squirmed restlessly in my arms, clutching at his clothes, as though he wanted to get them off but didn't have the strength or presence of mind to do it himself.

"Don't worry, Mr. Curry, I've got you," I said, hurrying to my usual room at the end of the hall.

I was glad for the familiar surroundings once I got into the room, because Mr. Curry was not only in a state himself, he had my head spinning with lust as well. The young man was one lollipop that I couldn't wait to lick all over until I was sticky with the man's slick and cum.

I had to shake my head again to clear my mind of dirty thoughts. I was a professional. I was here to serve the omega, not to live out my own fantasies. My client was in distress, and it was my duty to ease the young man's discomfort.

The fact that I was suddenly looking forward to the next three days like I'd never looked forward to a heat call before was completely irrelevant.

Ty

Mr. Curry hadn't stopped shaking from the moment I picked him up in the vestibule. He was still trembling desperately as I walked him to the king-size bed and gently laid him down.

"It's alright, Mr. Curry," I cooed again as the omega whimpered and squirmed and tried to cling to me. "It's just for a moment. I'm right here. I'm not going anywhere."

I didn't know what made me do it, since kissing was not something I did much of when on a heat call, but I bent down and touched my lips to Mr. Curry's plaintive, shapely mouth. I told myself it was an attempt to calm the young man down, but when Mr. Curry grasped my broad shoulders desperately and opened his mouth, begging for something deeper than just a peck, I couldn't help myself.

The young omega tasted as good as he smelled. I had to fight not to ravish the man. Or let myself tease my tongue into

Mr. Curry's mouth, tasting just enough of his sweetness to appease the groaning, desperate omega.

I shouldn't have been surprised by the greedy way Mr. Curry latched onto my tongue, kissing me back with enough need to sink a ship. I let out a deep, feral growl and leaned heavily on the bed beside the man, savaging his mouth with a kiss that got out of hand before I knew what had happened. I sucked and nipped, drinking in the taste and feeling of the helpless omega under me, his helplessness fueling my lust. The constraint of my jeans was beyond uncomfortable.

But I had a protocol to observe, and I damn well needed to do it fast.

"I know, baby, I know," I panted and cooed as I pulled back.

That right there should have alarmed me. I never called clients cute names. It just wasn't me. It wasn't part of the routine.

I backed away from the bed, despite Mr. Curry's whining and the way he reached for me.

"We have to observe the Bangers & Mash protocol, Mr. Curry," I said, heading for where I'd dropped the heat kit. I'd worry about my own bag later. "You signed the contracts digitally, but I need to go over the questions with you," I said, returning to the bed with the kit.

I unzipped it and searched its contents, and when that wasn't fast enough to get the laminated card with the ESA protocol on it out, I upended the thing and dumped its contents over the end of the bed. Two of the cans of specially formulated energy drink rolled off the bed, along with a bottle of lube, but I ignored them, grabbing at the protocol card.

Mr. Curry writhed on the bed beside where I sat, clawing at his clothes, but without enough coordination to remove them. The poor omega's skin was flushed, and even though he'd opened his eyes more than they had been downstairs, I could see his pupils were shot. And that they were blue. A very pretty blue at that.

I leaned into the man, ready to throw protocol out the window. At the last minute, the tiny shred of professionalism I was hanging onto prevailed.

"I know it doesn't seem important right now, but I can assure you, we need to go through these questions," I said.

"Please," Mr. Curry panted, his voice a soft tenor. "Please, help me."

I teetered on the verge of absolutely losing it. Mr. Curry smelled like lazy summertime days, before responsibility had pressed down on me. And he moaned like he needed my thick alpha cock buried in him so deeply that it breeched his womb. It didn't help at all that the seat of his jeans was definitely soaked through.

I cleared my throat, my hands shaking as I held the protocol card. I knew the questions like I knew my own name, but I couldn't remember them in that moment to save my life. I had to read from the card, which should have been a huge red flag.

"Do you confirm that you requested an Emergency Support Alpha from Bangers & Mash?"

Mr. Curry groaned and squirmed, pulling at his hoodie without any real strength or coordination.

"Mr. Curry?" I looked at him with concern, desperate to help—desperate to tear the young man's clothes off and spread his ass wide enough to let the heat slick flow out of him like a fountain, was more like it—but bound by the rules I'd followed for ten years. "Mr. Curry, do you confirm that you requested an Emergency Support Alpha from Bangers & Mash?" I asked again.

"Please," Mr. Curry panted. "Please!"

I chose to take that as a yes. My breath came in shorter

gasps as I asked the second question. "Do you consent to allowing me to take you through your heat?"

"Help me, please! It hurts!" Mr. Curry cried.

I definitely considered that a yes. I knew we were running out of time, so I moved on to the third question. "Do you acknowledge and accept that this will mean having intense sexual relations, including penetration and ejaculation?"

Mr. Curry wailed wordlessly. He somehow found the strength to push himself to a sitting position, then promptly threw himself at me. "It hurts so bad!" Tears streamed down the young omega's face.

How long had the man waited before coming to the hotel, and why hadn't he called me sooner? He'd obviously been in heat for hours already. I couldn't imagine the distress that was causing him.

And then the omega met my eyes directly. The poor man was weeping. Tears made his long, dark lashes clump together, and the thin blue iris around his blown pupils shone with need.

I sucked in a breath, then did something I'd never done in ten years. I tossed the protocol card aside and pulled Mr. Curry into my arms.

"I'm here, baby," I murmured before slanting my mouth over the young omega's.

It was like the entire purpose of my being coalesced into that single moment. That was why I was there. Mr. Curry was likely inexperienced. In his pre-heat interview, he said he'd had two heats before, but I doubted either of them were like this. My whole heart and soul told me that this was why I did what I did—to care for and protect omegas who were rendered helpless by biology.

I kissed Mr. Curry until we were both breathless and I was dizzy. As I did, I reached for the bottom of Mr. Curry's hoodie, sweeping it up and taking the t-shirt he wore under it with me.

As soon as I bared the omega's torso, a burst of scent wafted off him that was so strong I nearly blacked out with the intensity. It was so powerful that I nudged the man to his back as soon as I threw his shirt and hoodie aside, then bent over to press my open mouth to the warm flesh of the man's shoulders and chest. I kissed my way along the line of Mr. Curry's collarbone, then down to the omega's nipples.

The young man cried out when I closed my mouth around one nipple to lick and suck it. Omegas had sensitive nipples in the best of times, but during heat, they became so sensitive to touch that I had been known to make a client come just from playing with his nipples.

I had a feeling that that was exactly what Mr. Curry did when the young man bucked up with a loud cry as I sucked on one nipple and pinched the other gently. Sure enough, when I continued kissing my way down the omega's torso, dipping my tongue into the man's navel, and across the plane of his belly all the way to the waist of his jeans, a wet spot had formed on the front to match the soaked crotch.

"We need to get you out of these," I growled, fumbling with the fly of Mr. Curry's jeans.

I unbuttoned them and pulled the fly down, then tugged the ruined fabric. Right away, Mr. Curry's cock leapt free, already hard again after coming. It wasn't unusual. Omegas tended to produce less fluid than alphas, even in heat, but they orgasmed almost constantly throughout heat waves, especially on the first and second day of heat.

That was just routine knowledge to me. What wasn't routine at all was the beauty of Mr. Curry's body. His cock was average in size and his balls a little on the small side, but the perfection of the lines of his body as I tugged his jeans, underwear and shoes off and left him bare and writhing on top of the bed was second to none.

I had seen more than my fair share of naked omegas in heat in my day, but Mr. Curry truly was extraordinary. He had the graceful shape and slight muscle tone of a dancer. Omegas didn't grow much hair in general, but Mr. Curry had enough around his groin to indicate he was a man and not a boy. Other than that, his chest was hairless, and his nipples stood pert and pink, begging for more attention.

But it was the shining gush of slick that spilled from Mr. Curry's hole as he drew his legs up and tilted his hips in offering that had my blood pounding through me. He was already so impossibly wet that I pulsed to lose myself in those hot, slick depths.

"Please," Mr. Curry begged and wept. "Oh, God, please. I need…I need…."

"Shh, sweetheart, I've got you," I growled, already tugging off the plain t-shirt I wore.

If it was possible, Mr. Curry's pupils got even bigger as he watched me undress by the side of the bed. Mr. Curry had a typical omega physique, and I was textbook alpha. I was over six feet and broad as an oak, even though I didn't work out half as much as some other alphas I knew. My chest was hairy and defined, and a line of hair ran over my tight abs to the waist of my jeans. I unbuttoned those jeans in a hurry and shoved them down, toeing off my shoes as I did.

When I kicked them aside and stood, my long, thick cock stood up, already shining with precum on its flared tip. Mr. Curry moaned, his eyes seeming to lose sight entirely as he thrashed on the bedcovers.

"Please, please, please," he panted, like it was a prayer and I was the only one who could answer it. He grabbed his legs under his knees and pulled himself up as if to give me everything.

It did not help my control one bit to see the attractive young man spread and gushing, like some sort of offering. I wasn't proud of the fact that the omega's tears triggered something fierce and primal in me. My clients almost never cried. They always understood why they were there and what they should expect. I'd never had anyone wait so long before being taken through their heat, though, so anything could happen.

"I'm here," I managed to say, though my words came out with a tinge of alpha threat to them instead of with my usual professional calm. "Let's just prep a few things and then I'll—"

"No!" Mr. Curry wailed. "Now! Now! I need you now!" His words devolved into sobs.

Fuck courtesy and keeping the bedspread clean. Fuck getting Mr. Curry more comfortable. Between the overpowering omega scent and Mr. Curry's tears and the way he was offering himself so desperately, and between my own soul-deep need to have this omega, right here, right now, there was no stopping things.

It was a minor miracle that I was able to grab the box of alpha condoms that had spilled out of the heat kit when I'd upended it. If the box had fallen off the bed, I probably wouldn't have bothered. But the one, tiny, final shred of professionalism that I still had in me demanded that I tear the box apart and rip open a packet with shaking hands, then frantically roll it over my painfully hard dick.

Mr. Curry watched the whole process, panting so hard that I was afraid he might pass out. Every inch of his pale skin was flushed pink, and his gaping hole dripped with slick, pulsing slightly, as though it were hungry for me.

I was certainly hungry for it. I practically dove into the omega, lifting the young man's legs over his shoulders, then bending down to bring my mouth to that glistening hole. Mr. Curry cried out as I licked across his hole, causing more slick to pour out like the juicy center of a filled candy, then plunged my tongue inside.

I felt, rather than saw, Mr. Curry come a second time. The omega's ass clenched with the orgasm as I tongued it and groaned with possessive pride. In the back of my mind, I was surprised with myself for having such a strong reaction, but it just felt right. For the time being, Mr. Curry was mine. I almost never let my alpha rear his head that way when I was with a client, but it was as if I couldn't stop myself.

Something was different about Mr. Curry. Something in his scent and the tightness of his hole as he came a third time before I realized it. The young man was wild with pleasure, but that was what happened when an omega waited too long before doing anything about their heat.

A warning tightness in my balls and at the base of my cock pushed me to move. I lifted myself above Mr. Curry, staring down at the thin spurts of cum that now painted his belly, and wondered what it was that made this particular heat different from the hundreds of others I'd helped with.

Even that question was blown out of my mind when Mr. Curry's eyes went wide at the sight of me towering over him, and he went from holding his knees wide to gripping my arms. "Please, oh, please," the distressed omega gasped. "I need you in me! I need it!"

"I know, baby," I answered.

I wasted no more time in lifting Mr. Curry's hips and positioning my own cock at the man's soaked entrance. With one smooth push, I slid into all that pulsing heat and wetness. Mr. Curry was tight. Very tight. So much so that I adjusted my strategy and rocked in and out, pushing a bit deeper each time as the omega gasped and moaned and wailed. Two prior heats or not, I could feel that the young man had had very little sexual experience.

That point was underscored even more when I went deep

enough to enter his breeding passage. Mr. Curry let out a shout and gripped my sides so tightly I was sure to have bruises later.

"Do you want me to stop?" I asked, taking my cues from Mr. Curry's body. "Is it too much?"

Mr. Curry groaned and grunted, his face contorted with the unique sort of pleasure-pain that omegas sometimes felt when they'd waited too long and had to be fucked through the cramps before truly enjoying how good heat sex felt.

I started to pull out, intending to give the man a rest, but Mr. Curry's eyes flew wide, and he wailed, "No!" He clutched at me and even bore down on me to keep me from pulling away.

That was all the consent I needed.

"I've got you, sweetheart," I cooed, pushing deeper. "I'll make it better, I promise."

I resumed my gentle thrusts, slowly opening up Mr. Curry's body until his whimpers of pain and fright turned into guttural sounds of pleasure. The omega was beyond words, but I had more than enough experience to feel the muscles and organs in the young man's body loosen up as the heat cramps subsided.

What the young man really needed was for me to come inside him a few times. Hormones from alpha ejaculate were the only thing that could completely sate an omega in heat, and he would get to that once I had the presence of mind to break out the spermicide. In the meantime, the condom would have to do to stop Mr. Curry from becoming pregnant. That was the number one tenant of the B&M promise. The service was for omegas who did not want to become pregnant.

But for some reason, ten years of training away my alpha instincts flew out the window. As I judged it safe to thrust harder and deeper, and as Mr. Curry moaned and writhed with pleasure under me, that voice of alpha instinct within me begged me to spill everything I had into the young omega's womb and to fill him with my babies.

I ignored it as unprofessional, but that didn't stop me from thrusting hard and pumping right up against the entrance to Mr. Curry's womb. I generally saved that ultimate penetration for later in a heat, but I wanted to feel myself so deep in the beautiful, helpless omega under me with such a ferocious need that I grasped at what I wanted.

The tip of my cock breeched Mr. Curry's womb, and the young omega howled with pleasure, his whole body convulsing as the powerful heat orgasm shook him. I even reached between us to close my hand around the omega's cock as it pulsed and spilled with the intensity of the pleasure the young man was lost to.

"That's it, baby," I growled against the sweet-smelling omega's ear. "Come for me."

That command sent another wave of orgasm through Mr. Curry. That was the one that did it. As the omega arched into me, his womb squeezing around the head of my cock and more cum spilling between us, my knot formed with almost painful speed and intensity, locking our bodies together.

The accompanying orgasm was stronger than I had ever felt. It shot through me like thunder, feeling like it would turn me inside out. I was pretty sure I roared with the intensity of it, but for a moment, it was like I couldn't hear or see. All I could do was feel the pleasure that swallowed me whole, and feel the corresponding throb of my omega's body around me and in my arms. In that moment, we were one, wholly and completely.

I wasn't even sure how much time had passed before sense started to wash through me again, like the gentle, clearing rain at the end of a powerful storm. I felt so good that I let out a deep sigh of contentment and rolled to my side, taking my omega with me.

More sense returned to me, and I realized Mr. Curry was panting heavily, but that his body was relaxed and still. I adjusted a bit more on my side, lifting Mr. Curry's leg over my hip into what was hopefully a more comfortable position for him while we were knotted, and I tugged one of the pillows down so Mr. Curry could rest his head on it.

"Comfortable?" I asked, still catching my own breath.

Mr. Curry nodded. His body tensed just a bit, and when I looked at him with an assessing glance, the young man gazed back at me with wide, shell-shocked eyes.

"It's okay, Mr. Curry," I said. "It's not unusual to experience a moment of shock or embarrassment after that first wave. Especially since we didn't have as much time as usual to acclimate to each other before the heat wave started."

"What?" the omega asked, his voice a bit thin.

"Just breathe for a moment," I told him. "We'll go through the full protocol as soon as my knot goes down. It could be a few minutes, up to half an hour at most."

Mr. Curry squirmed a bit, bearing down and pulling away from my knot. The movement sent another small orgasm through him that had the omega groaning with pleasure, and a hint of fear.

"It's okay, Mr. Curry," I said, closing my arms around the omega. I even kissed the man's face a few times as an unusual burst of sentiment hit me. "Orgasms while knotted are very common for omegas. Enjoy them."

"Wh-why do you keep calling me that?" the young omega asked, looking at me as though he were afraid.

"Call you...what?" I suddenly wondered if I'd gone too far with the terms of endearments.

But the omega said, "Mr. Curry. Why do you keep calling me that?"

I blinked at him. The omega seemed completely lucid, now that the first wave was over and he'd been satisfied.

"Because it's your name?" I asked, even as a horrifying suspicion came over me. "Doyle Curry?"

The omega looked completely terrified. "That's not my name," he said in a hoarse whisper. "My name is Winslow. Winslow Grant."

I stared back at him, awkwardness and dread and pure shock spilling through me. Ten years without making a single mistake, and all of a sudden, I'd bedded the wrong omega.

Chapter Three

Winslow

It didn't matter how many videos I'd watched in Health class back in high school, or how many anecdotal stories my friends had told me about their own first heats—or those apocryphal horror stories of first heats that everyone seemed to know—nothing had prepared me for the full onslaught of everything a heat wave could do to me.

It had started sometime in the middle of the night. Those first stirrings of heat were strong enough to wake me from an exhausted sleep after a full day of dealing with Carl, and the landlord, and my boss—well, now my ex-boss—and Mrs. McCready in the apartment next door...who was complaining about Carl. The cramps woke me at around three in the morning, and despite my best attempts to ignore them and get a few more hours of sleep before what was sure to be another exhausting day of looking for a new job, heat got the best of me.

I honestly wasn't sure how I'd ended up where I was—in a hotel by the beach, I thought, in bed with the most gorgeous alpha I'd ever seen. The alpha looked to be at least ten years older than me. He was tall and muscled, had thick, brown hair that was tousled, but still managed to look perfect, deep brown eyes, and enough scruff on the lower half of his face to make him look dangerous. The man's chest and shoulders were broad and firm, his scent was like the forest after a hard rain, and—oh, God!—we were knotted!

Panic washed through me, and I squirmed as if I could get away.

"Shh, shh," the alpha tried to soothe and calm me. "It's okay. You're okay."

I was anything but okay. I should have known there was no getting away from the alpha. Not while we were knotted.

And, God, it felt good! The sheer terror of waking up in bed in the middle of heat with a stranger I was knotted with aside, the pleasure of having a knotted alpha cock buried deep inside me was every bit as incredible as I'd always heard it would be.

But that hardly made up for the shock of the situation.

"Who are you?" I demanded, hating how small and weak and panicky I sounded. "Where am I? How did I get here?"

Even though I knew it was futile, I wriggled a bit more to see if I could get away from the alpha. But moving with the man's knot inside me only caused bursts of pleasure that sent shudders through my whole body and made my eyes roll back in my head. I had to fight not to orgasm.

"It's okay," the alpha said once again, his voice deep and soothing. "Don't worry. There's been some sort of mistake, but I've got you. I'm not going to hurt you or let you go through this alone."

The alpha rolled me to my back, but was careful about the way he loomed over me with our bodies still joined. I had the impression the alpha had only done it to keep me from moving in a way that would cause me to hurt myself.

Slowly, I focused on the alpha's face, trying not to hyperventilate...or cry. Fuck. Sometimes I hated being an omega. It was a stupid stereotype that omegas were overly emotional and cried easily, but lately, all things with my fucked-up life considered, it was too true.

"There," the alpha said once I was breathing a little more normally and able to meet the man's eyes. "You're okay. I'm not going to hurt you. My name is Tybalt Martin, but everyone calls me Ty. I'm an Emergency Support Alpha. I work for Bangers & Mash, and I'm here at The Grand because I had a client."

I tried to grasp on to what the man said, but it took my heat-fogged brain a few minutes to process.

"Bangers & Mash," I said, blinking up at the gorgeous man. "That's that thing where rich omegas hire alphas to take them through their heat."

The alpha smiled. "We try to keep our services affordable for all omegas, but yes, that's the gist of it."

I squeezed his eyes shut, wincing. I was fucked. Literally and figuratively. I didn't have any money. No money at all. That was the problem with the landlord yesterday. I couldn't pay the rent, let alone hire an expensive ESA.

I popped my eyes open as another thought hit me. "I didn't hire you," I said, feeling and sounding guilty. "I don't know why you came to the hotel, but I didn't hire you. I couldn't. I'm not even sure how I got here."

The alpha frowned, sending another wave of panic through me. The man was pissed off, and I was in the most vulnerable position possible.

But the alpha said, "I was here for a client, a Mr. Curry, but you said your name was Winslow?"

"Winslow Grant," I said in a thready voice, turning my

head to look away, embarrassed. "I'm sorry. I didn't mean to cause trouble." And yet, I always did.

"Hey, it's okay," the alpha said. He slipped a hand under my cheek and nudged me to face him again. "Mistakes happen."

I blinked up at him. "Do they? You've gotten the wrong omega before?"

The alpha frowned a little. "Well, no. In ten years of doing this job, I never have."

I was ready to die of shame, but the alpha went on with, "You might not have been the client I came to the hotel to visit, but from the moment I saw you, I knew you were in extreme distress." He frowned again and asked, "When did your heat start? Why weren't you taking care of it some other way?"

I lowered my eyes in shame. The man had no idea how loaded the questions he was asking were.

I realized then that I'd been gripping the alpha's arms so tightly my fingertips were probably going to leave bruises. I let go, but with the way we were knotted, there wasn't much to do with my arms but let them flop back on the pillow by the sides of my head. Only, when I did that, something fierce and sexual filled the alpha's eyes, and I felt the man's body stiffen and heat up over mine.

Which caused every cell in my body to go from zero to a thousand on the horniness scale in half a second.

Not what I needed in that moment.

I shifted his arms to hold them straight down at my sides, but the damage had already been done. I was too aware of how horny both the alpha and I were getting, and all from just lying there.

But the alpha had asked me a question, and I owed it to the guy to answer.

"I woke up around three this morning already feeling it," I

mumbled, staring at a spot on the alpha's chest instead of looking him in the eyes. "I guess technically it could have started hours before that? I was kind of feeling off before going to bed last night around ten, but it was a crazy day and I was tired."

A long pause followed, as if the alpha expected more of an explanation. When I didn't give one, the alpha asked, "And you don't have a boyfriend or friend or heat toys to take you through?"

My embarrassment deepened. I shook my head, looking anywhere but in the alpha's eyes.

"What did you do for your last heat?" the alpha asked on.

I prayed for death. If I admitted to this huge, gorgeous, professional heat alpha that this was my first heat and that I hadn't known what to expect or what was happening to me, I was certain the man would laugh at me. That would probably kill me for sure. Only utter dweebs were unprepared for their first heat.

I was spared having to come up with some sort of answer when the alpha's knot suddenly started to go down. As much of a relief as it was for me to be able to wiggle away from the man as our bodies separated, it also felt like someone was pulling one of my limbs off. Not in terms of pain, but every part of my insides was convinced that the alpha belonged inside me.

That didn't stop me from shuffling away and curling into a ball once I was free.

The alpha rocked back and sat staring at me for a moment. Of course, that enabled me to stare right back at him. Or rather, to stare at the alpha's enormous cock, which was still half hard in the condom that sheathed it and glistening with my slick. I was simultaneously struck with disbelief that something so big could fit inside of me and embarrassed to my core that I'd produced—strike that, was still producing—so much slick.

"I need to call my office," the alpha said, moving off the bed, carefully removing the condom—which looked impossibly full—and bending for his jeans, which were on the floor.

Actually, a lot of stuff was on the floor around the bed—the alpha's clothes, my clothes, and a bunch of random stuff, like energy drinks and...and packages of baby wipes?

"Feel free to use the bathroom if you need to," the alpha said as he pulled a cellphone from the back pocket of his jeans. "You can even take a shower if you want, although chances are another heat wave will hit you soon. The hotel always stocks these rooms with bottled water and snacks, if you feel you need something."

What I needed was a time machine so I could go back and figure out how to get through this whole thing without ending up in a hotel room with a complete stranger who was bigger and older than me.

"Thanks," I muttered instead and slipped off the bed.

I skittered to the bathroom, mortified at the sheer volume of slick leaking from me as I moved. It could have been worse, though. I could have been leaking alpha cum along with—

My thought stopped short as a shudder of longing passed through me. I wanted alpha cum all over me, inside and out. It was like the strongest craving I'd ever felt. If I didn't get stuffed with alpha cum immediately, I was going to die.

I took a deep breath and continued on to the toilet. At least I had enough sense to know that was my omega biology talking. But there was a huge difference between watching a cheesy video with a chirpy omega talking about how every part of omega biology was designed to encourage pregnancy and actually experiencing it.

I used the toilet, then washed my face and brushed my teeth, then donned the complimentary hotel robe hanging behind the door before heading back to the main part of the hotel room. I grabbed a bottle of water from the room's table, but I didn't know what to do as the alpha continued his call.

"Yeah, I know," the alpha said as he paced the room. Paced the room naked, I noticed. Just watching him had me getting hard and wet all over again. "I just feel bad is all," he told whoever he was talking to, sounding deeply disappointed in himself. There was another pause before he said, "Really? He's willing to do that? Hamish just took a call. Is he ready for another one?"

I felt awkward for listening to something that wasn't any of my business, but I didn't have anywhere to go, other than walking over to peek out the window.

That's when I realized we must have been on the top floor of The Grand, which was one of Barrington's most expensive beachside hotels.

A different sort of panic overtook me. I couldn't afford to be in the situation I was in. I couldn't afford an ESA, and I definitely couldn't afford The Grand. What was I going to do? When the alpha found out, he would—

"Winslow, are you okay?" the alpha asked, right behind me.

I yelped, nearly dropping my water bottle, and jerked around to face the alpha.

Who was close. So close. I breathed in the man's fresh forest scent and felt a gush of slick spill out of me and trickle down my thigh. I felt flushed and restless all over again, and it took everything I had not to plaster myself against the alpha and hump him into oblivion.

"I'm sorry," I gasped, starting to shake. "This is all my fault. I should have known what was happening. I should have planned better. Now I've messed everything up for you, and I don't have any money to pay you or to pay for the hotel, and I—"

"Shh, it's okay, baby."

I would have snapped my gaze up to gape at the man, but he'd closed the small gap between us and wrapped his arms around me.

I groaned with relief and arousal before I could stop myself, pulling off the hotel robe as I did. I couldn't stand to have anything but an alpha against my skin anymore. God, no one ever mentioned how embarrassing heat was.

"I've got you," the alpha said, picking me up.

Like a complete slut, I wrapped my legs around the alpha's waist and wriggled my ass over the man's cock. The alpha sucked in a breath as though the crude seduction technique might actually work.

"I'm not going to abandon you while you're in heat," the alpha said as he walked me back to the bed. "Even though this was a mistake, you need me. I'm going to take you through your heat, and I'm not going to charge you."

I whimpered and clung to the man like a monkey as he peeled back the bedcovers, then sank into the cool sheets, carrying me with him.

"Bangers & Mash has an arrangement with the hotel, so you don't need to worry about that cost either," the alpha went on, rocking back long enough to gather some of the things that had been strewn across the bed and repositioning them to the pillow beside where my head lay. "I'm going to be with you the whole time, making this as easy and pleasurable as possible," the alpha went on. "I don't want you to worry about a thing. And I don't want you to feel ashamed either. This is all very normal for heat, okay?"

There was no chance in hell that I wouldn't feel deeply embarrassed through my entire heat, but I nodded and grunted all the same. I was past the point of being able to talk, though.

The alpha reached for one of the bottles he'd placed on the

pillow as he knelt between my obscenely spread legs. It was all I could do to pay attention to the alpha's words and not his erect, dripping cock as he said, "We didn't have a chance to go through the whole protocol or to discuss how you want to handle your heat, but I feel like you need the comfort you'll get from alpha ejaculate in you. So if you consent, we'll use this specially formulated spermicide to prevent pregnancy. I usually advise my clients to go on the pill before—"

"Yes!" I shouted, the prospect of the alpha coming inside me drowning out all other thoughts. "Use that. Come in me. Come all over me. I'll suck your cock and drink it."

I had no idea where that thought came from, but I was beyond even being embarrassed about it. I'd only attempted to give a blow job a handful of times and they had been disasters, but I would choke on the alpha's fat cock and not care if it meant I had cum in me.

"Okay," the alpha said, sounding annoyingly calm, considering how desperate I was starting to feel. "We'll go with the spermicide for a few waves until the chemical effects of—"

"Now!" I growled, scrambling to flip to my hands and knees and presenting my gushing hole to the alpha. "Please, please just give it to me now! I feel like I'm going to die."

Maybe that was an exaggeration, but it didn't feel like it in the moment. I moved my knees wider and lowered my head and shoulders to the bed, keening wildly and waving my wide-open ass at the alpha. It was horrible and humiliating. I felt like a stereotype of every omega porno I'd ever watched. But I also felt as though my body had one purpose and one purpose only—I was a hole for an alpha to fuck, and that was it.

"It's okay," the alpha said, accompanied by the sound of a bottle snapping open and a squirt as its contents were squeezed out. "I know this feels awkward and embarrassing, but I can assure you that you're perfectly normal. This is absolutely ordinary for early heat waves."

I wanted to snap some sort of snarky retort, but when the alpha's fingers slipped into my pulsing hole, spreading what felt like ice-cold gel inside of me, I came all over the sheets.

It was just a small orgasm, if there was such a thing, but a few seconds later, when the wide head of the alpha's cock pressed against my hole, then stretched me to the point where I cried out with the insane mix of pleasure and pain and completeness that action brought with it as he pushed slowly inside, I started coming harder.

Everything blurred together at that point. Orgasm after orgasm rocked my body as the alpha thrust deeper and deeper into me. I could feel every inch of that thick cock filling me and claiming me. It was like having an oak pushed into me, but it felt so good that I wanted to disappear into the sensation. I even rocked back hard in time with the alpha's thrust, fucking myself on that monster cock until I could feel the tip push into the center of my soul.

Logically, I knew the sensation was the alpha breeching my womb, but fuck logic. The orgasm that hit me was like being turned inside out with pleasure, having every cell in my body transformed into flashing heart emojis, then having each of those emojis burst into flame. It consumed me completely, and when I heard the alpha start to growl and groan, and as the man's cum started to fill me, it was like I turned into pure, liquid sex.

It might have been one of the most humiliating moments of my life, but as I slipped into a state of near nirvana as the alpha embraced me with his whole body, his knot swelling to lock us together in mind-numbing pleasure, I felt like heat was definitely something I could get used to.

Ty

One of the things about being an ESA that I had always been told, and that I taught in my ESA training classes, was that no two heat support calls were the same. But what I'd always tried to downplay in teaching was that some of those calls were way more intense than others.

It was only the second heat wave, but I was already certain that this accidental call with Winslow Grant was going to go down as the most intense call I'd ever taken.

I rolled to my side, taking Winslow with me as gently as I could after coming so hard right into the young omega's womb that I'd nearly blacked out. My knot throbbed in the impossibly tight sheath of Winslow's body, joining us physically, but as I closed my arms around the blissed-out young man, pulling Winslow's back against my sweaty chest so I could hold him as we came back to earth, I felt joined to Winslow on other levels as well.

I had so many questions, but I needed to give Winslow a moment to piece his brain back together. I had enough experience with omegas in heat to know that particular wave and the deep orgasm Winslow had experienced had consumed the young man to the point where he would need a few minutes to recover. I could still feel the occasional twitch and tremor as secondary orgasms continued to work their way through the omega's body.

I smiled, indulging in a bit of pride in my work for giving the omega so much pleasure. Then again, an omega's capacity to experience pleasure during heat—or just having sex outside of heat—was greatly dependent on his or her own willingness to get out of their head and into their bodies and to let go. Winslow was very good at letting go and allowing his body to take over.

I leaned in and kissed the back of the young man's neck. I shouldn't have done it. The gesture was too informal for what I was used to. But something about Winslow's obvious vulnerability and the fear that had been in his eyes when he'd realized the situation he was in had touched me. In my ten years of helping omegas through heat I'd had a few clients who had been nervous at first, but I'd never ended up with an omega who was genuinely terrified. The fact that Winslow hadn't intended to end up with me at all explained that, but it was still new to me.

Actually, the fact that, despite his fear, Winslow had been able to let go enough during his heat waves to have orgasms that intense was a testament to how strong his character was. Thinking about that had me wondering what Winslow was like in the rest of his life, what sort of personality he had, what things he loved and gave his heart to.

Those thoughts earned the sweet omega another few kisses on the back of his neck. That overpowering lollipop scent had me wanting to lick him as well.

My tongue was already against Winslow's neck when I forced myself to stop and come to my senses. Winslow Grant was a client. He was an accidental client, but a client all the same. That meant I had to be professional and not scare the young man by licking him when he was in a stupor.

But Winslow groaned and wriggled against me and mumbled, "Why did you stop?"

A moment later, Winslow jerked in my arms, tensing as if he'd heard his own question and it had startled him.

"How are you feeling?" I asked. My voice sounded somehow more tender than it ever had, but that could have been my imagination.

"Humiliated," Winslow said, burying his face in the pillow. He ground his hips against mine, probably testing to see whether we were still knotted. We were, and the gesture ended up sending another, small orgasm through Winslow that had him catching his breath and moaning with pleasure.

"Shh. Hold still, baby," I said. I caught my breath and blinked at my inadvertent use of the pet name. Again. I really needed to stop doing that. I covered the slip by rushing on with, "Like I said, there's nothing at all to be ashamed of. You're behaving like a normal, healthy, young omega."

Winslow kept his face buried in the pillow, as if he were trying to avoid looking at me completely. My chest constricted at the thought that my omega—that is, my client—felt so embarrassed by what was completely normal. I stroked Winslow's dark, sweaty hair back from his forehead, then drew my hand down Winslow's arm in long, soothing strokes. That seemed to calm Winslow a bit...and also to send tremors of feather-light orgasms through the omega's body.

"What were your first few heats like?" I asked. Making conversation while knotted often put an anxious omega at ease.

Instead, Winslow tensed, and not in a good way. He

turned his head slowly and glanced up at me over his shoulder with the most bashful look I had ever seen. Even before Winslow spoke, my heart started racing.

"Um," Winslow said, then mumbled, "this is my first heat."

My chest constricted so hard I thought my heart might stop. Instead, it raced even more. "Your first heat?" I repeated.

Winslow nodded, his face bright red, and buried his face in the pillow again. He mumbled something into the pillow that I didn't catch.

"What was that?" I asked, holding the young man closer and stroking his side and hip.

Winslow dragged his head around to look up at me again, but he couldn't hold my gaze for more than a second as he murmured, "It was actually my first time."

I blinked. "Your...your first time...having sex?"

Winslow nodded and buried his face in the pillow again, his whole body heating.

I caught my breath. Something inside me roared with a kind of possessive protectiveness that went beyond all my experience. It was so strong that it rattled me.

"Bab—er, Winslow, I'm sorry," I said, fighting the tendrils of guilty panic that tried to coil through me. "If I'd've known...."

I let that futile thought drop. What happened, happened. There was no erasing it now. And honestly, I didn't think I wanted to. As far as I knew, I'd never taken anyone's virginity. At least I'd made it enjoyable for Winslow, even if my omega— er, my client—no, just Winslow—even if he'd been too heat-addled that first time to really know what was going on.

"How do you feel?" I asked again, falling back on protocol to cover the tumultuous feelings that were trying to overtake the professionalism I knew I needed to maintain. "Do you have any unusual discomfort?"

Winslow laughed wryly and twisted to look at me again. "Discomfort other than having a strange alpha's massive cock so far up my ass that I can feel your heartbeat in my womb?" he asked.

Despite everything, I grinned at Winslow's snark. I even laughed, which was definitely not something I did with clients.

My laughter caused movement that had Winslow sucking in a breath and rolling his eyes back in his head. Another small orgasm hit him, and he moaned. "Fuck, that feels good," he managed to say as it subsided. "They definitely don't talk about how good this feels in Health class."

I sucked in a breath. "Um, Winslow, how old are you?" I asked, visions of losing my license for taking an underaged omega through heat suddenly swimming in my head.

"Twenty," Winslow muttered, hiding his face again.

I let out a breath of relief. Twenty was definitely legal. Although, I understood Winslow's sheepishness over admitting his age. He was a late-bloomer. It wasn't unheard of for an omega to experience his first heat as late as twenty, but eighteen was more usual.

"I'm thirty-one," I told him, figuring Winslow had a right to know.

"Okay," Winslow said, relaxing a little. "Um, thanks for telling me."

"It was only fair," I said. "We should talk between heat waves," I went on, compelled to know more about my ome—dammit, I needed to stop thinking that way. "I usually know a lot more about clients before their heats actually start. We conduct interviews at B&M, sometimes in person, sometimes by video chat."

"So how come you thought I was that... Mr. Curry?" Winslow glanced up at me, as if checking whether he'd gotten the name right.

I nodded. "Curry, yes. He's a second-year medical student at Barrington University, and we only conducted interviews over email because of his busy schedule."

And that was about ten times more information than I should have been divulging about a client. What was wrong with me? Mistaking Winslow for a client, calling him pet names, kissing him between heats, and now letting private information about another client just spill out of me?

Something was definitely off.

No sooner had that thought hit me than my knot started to go down. As that happened, Winslow's body naturally drifted away from mine. And that was another thing. I was usually more than ready for my knot to go down so I could get some space from a client, enough to breathe for a few minutes at least. As Winslow wriggled away from me, I felt almost...bereft?

"I have to pee again," Winslow mumbled, scrambling away from me, all awkward arms and legs. "I don't usually have to go like this."

"It's normal," I reassured him, back to official ESA manners. "The activity of heat waves tends to irritate internal organs, like the bladder." Translation—I'd pounded Winslow's ass so hard during that last wave that everything in his abdomen probably felt like it'd been hit with a two-by-four.

"Um, okay," Winslow said, his beautiful face bright pink and his lovely blue eyes downcast. He met my eyes for a moment before looking away again and stumbling toward the bathroom. "I'll just...." He didn't finish his sentence before turning and running, shutting the bathroom door behind him.

I let out a heavy sigh and flopped to my back. I rubbed my face, pressing the heels of my hands against my eyes. I'd never screwed up before, but when I did, I screwed up royally. Here I was, trying to tell Winslow everything was normal, but the things I was feeling, physically and emotionally, definitely weren't normal.

It was the unusual nature of the situation, I told myself as I climbed out of bed and reached for one of the packets of wipes from the heat kit. I was feeling off because the call had gone wrong, that was all.

Although that didn't explain why I felt the need to wipe some of Winslow's slick from my groin with my fingers, then to suck on those fingers instead of using the wipes. The sweet taste was so good that I groaned and closed my eyes, savoring the remnants of my ome—nope, not going there.

I was spared from having to analyze why the taste of Winslow's slick had my dick going hard by the sound of my phone binging with a text message. A few seconds later, it binged again. I ripped open the wipes and cleaned up as best I could before setting the pack on the bedside table, tossing the used wipes in the trash, then reaching for my phone, also on the bedside table.

But when I looked at it, there were no messages. Another bing sounded, and it dawned on me that Winslow must have had a phone too. That brought to my attention the fact that all our clothes still littered the floor. I set to work picking things up, folding them, and setting everything on top of the room's dresser.

In the process, Winslow's phone fell out of the pocket of his hoodie and hit the floor. As I bent to pick it up, another message binged, and when I turned the phone towards my face, it lit up, showing all four messages.

"Who doesn't have a password on his phone?" I wondered aloud. I would need to give Winslow a stern lecture about phone security—except Winslow wasn't my responsibility beyond the duration of his heat.

The content of the four text messages changed my mind about that assumption in an instant.

Any luck?

Did you find someone to buy your heat?

How much did you get for it?

If you're not answering because you're mad at me, get over it. We need the money, Winslow. Swallow your pride, and some alpha cock, and get us that rent money.

As I read the last message, seeing red over what I was reading, a fifth message came in.

Seriously, get it over with and get back here as fast as possible. You can be pissed off at me later.

"What are you doing?" Winslow asked from the bathroom door just as I was contemplating calling whoever was texting Winslow to give them a piece of my mind.

Instead, I turned to Winslow—who had a towel around his waist, even though it was clear he hadn't taken a shower—held the phone out to him, and asked, "Are you in danger? Is this some sort of domestic abuse situation?"

Winslow looked momentarily horrified, then marched across the room and grabbed the phone from me. He let out a breath and his eyes went wide as he read the texts. "Carl," he whispered, as if the name were a curse.

The sheer ferocity of the protectiveness that I felt had me teetering on the edge of actually roaring—which was not just ridiculous, it wouldn't have been remotely helpful.

"Is Carl your boyfriend?" I asked instead, and because Winslow hadn't answered the first time, I asked again, "Are you in an abusive household?"

Winslow scowled at his phone as he typed something then said, with more annoyance than fear, "No, not at all. Carl is my brother, and he's...he's Carl." He sighed heavily and shook his head, then finished typing a message, then hit send.

There were about fifty things I wanted to say, but I settled on, "Selling your heat is a big deal, Winslow. Selling your first heat is an even bigger one."

"Trust me, I know," Winslow said with just enough sass to put Ty at ease. "And I wasn't going to do it. No matter what arguments Carl tried to make. I just thought...." His gaze lost its focus as his words faded. I had the feeling he was remembering something, especially when Winslow glanced back to me with a guilty look, blushing. "I remember how I got to the hotel," he mumbled.

"Do you want to tell me?" I asked. I intended it to be a gentle, genuine question, but I ended up crossing my arms, leaning against the dresser, and snapping the question, as if Winslow owed me an answer, which he absolutely did not.

Winslow clutched his phone with one hand and rubbed his free hand over his hair. He peeked sheepishly up at me and said, "I was going to just go somewhere, tough it out through my heat, then go home and tell Carl I couldn't find anyone to pay me." He swallowed. "Then it got really bad. I...I wasn't thinking clearly, but I came to the hotel because I thought I might be able to find someone to pay me for it here." When I scowled, Winslow rushed on with, "I wasn't thinking clearly. I would never ask someone for money in exchange for sex. It's just—"

"I know," I cut him off. Not only was Winslow genuinely agitated at the suggestion he would prostitute his heat, I knew full well how desperate he'd been that morning.

I pushed away from the dresser, crossed to the table where the water bottles sat, and took one. I then headed to the foot of the bed and sat, gesturing for Winslow to come sit with me.

"Tell me about this brother of yours, Carl," I said. "You said it was his idea for you to sell your heat?"

Winslow wavered for a moment before walking to sit on the bed, keeping a little distance between the two of us. The way he sat, with his shoulders hunched, made him look younger than twenty years old. Which raised all sorts of feelings in me that were entirely inappropriate for the situation.

At last, Winslow let out a breath and said, "Carl is my older brother. Older by two years. He's a beta. Our mom was a single mother, but she died of cancer three years ago."

"I'm sorry," I said, my alpha going nuts with protectiveness to the point where I had to grip the bedcovers with my free hand to stop myself from pulling Winslow into my embrace.

Winslow shrugged. "Carl was old enough when Mom died to take care of me without the two of us being put in foster care, but he's sort of...." Winslow winced. "He's not a bad guy, but I've always ended up taking care of him. He's...he's one of those people who is filled with big ideas, but he doesn't have the patience to make anything work out. Like, he's got bad ADHD or something."

"Has he ever been tested?" I asked.

"When he was a kid, I think," Winslow said. "I don't really know. Anyhow, I got a job right out of high school to pay the rent, and it's not that Carl doesn't try to get jobs, he just doesn't...show up." Winslow hunched in on himself even more. "He's shown up at my jobs a couple of times and gotten me fired in the process. I really thought this last job was going to stick, but...." He swallowed, then glanced to me with the most mournful, miserable expression I had ever seen. "I was fired yesterday. And the rent is past due. And then this heat thing happened, and Carl thought it was the answer to our prayers."

He finished his story in a mumble, looking dejectedly at his phone as he held it in his lap.

I was beside myself as all of the pieces of Winslow's story came together in my mind. My omega had been handed far too heavy a load for someone that young to bear. But he was strong. I knew it in the core of my being, even though

Winslow sat there, curled in on himself with defeat. He was a fighter, a survivor—not only for himself, but for this asshole brother of his. Winslow was as tough as nails, and he'd been prepared to do whatever it took to protect himself and his family. He might have looked like a beautiful, svelte omega on the surface, but he had the soul of a lion.

My instincts to protect and to shelter, to provide and save my omega—and dammit, I really needed to stop doing that, I was a professional, for Christ's sake—was overwhelming. I shifted on the bed to face Winslow more fully and was about to reach for him, but Winslow's phone rang.

All it took was a glimpse of the word "Carl" showing up on caller ID, and my calm good sense flew out the window.

As Winslow answered the call with, "Hey, what do you want?" I held out my hand with a furious scowl.

It was a silent demand, but Winslow's eyes went wide, and much to my surprise, he handed the phone over without a second thought.

"...running out of time before we're—"

"Are you Winslow's brother?" I cut off the fast-talking man on the other end of the call.

There was a choked silence, then Carl answered, "Yeah? Who is this?"

"This is Tybalt Martin, and you had better have a damn good reason for sending your brother out in such a vulnerable state or you'll have me to answer to."

Chapter Five

Winslow

I had no idea why I'd handed my phone over to a virtual stranger in the middle of Carl complaining to me about how bad things were for him. Carl was my problem to solve, not that of an alpha I'd just met. But Tybalt Martin exuded a kind of calm that had been missing from my life for the past three years, and even though the man hadn't said anything specific, I felt like I'd heard the alpha say "I'll take care of this" loud and clear.

And it felt better than sex.

Okay, well, not quite, but still.

After Ty's initial snap, there was a long silence, in which I could just make out the sound of Carl's voice arguing his point of view on the other end of the line. I shifted slightly, inching away from the alpha. I just stared at the man as Ty said, "Uh-huh," into the phone, as though he didn't believe a word Carl was saying.

There was a lot to stare at. Alphas were all big. That was just a fact of nature. Just like omegas, like me, were all small. Ty seemed to loom larger than most, although that might have had something to do with his expression as he listened to Carl ramble on. It was more than just Ty's firm, corded muscles or the width of his shoulders. Or the size of his thigh muscles, which I was trying hard not to look at, since that would inevitably lead me to stare at other large alpha things.

Things I wanted to get my hands on.

And my mouth.

Fuck. I should not be thinking about wrapping my lips around a virtual stranger's dick when the stranger in question was yelling at my brother, but the urge to drop to my knees and suck Ty into the back of my throat was almost overpowering.

"Yeah?" Ty barked, loud and sudden enough to snap me out of my thoughts. "Well, I don't care how difficult things are for you. Sending your brother out when he's in heat, expecting him to sell himself in order to make up for your irresponsible actions is abhorrent."

I blinked, then stared at Ty with open eyes. For an alpha who had fucked me twice now and made me come all over the place, he sure did use big words.

Then again, the little I knew about Ty kind of supported the idea that he was a professional. I didn't know a lot about Bangers & Mash, but I did know they weren't some fly-by-night organization that messed around with omegas, like some of the underground clubs I'd also heard about. B&M was the real deal. Which was why I would never in a million years be able to afford everything Ty was doing for me now.

I reminded myself that Ty had told me I wouldn't have to pay as Carl's voice rose on the other end of the call. Even with that offer, I felt terrible, especially considering the extra trouble I'd dumped on the kind alpha's doorstep with Carl.

"I'm the man who is actually helping your brother, which, I'm beginning to see, you haven't done much of," Ty said, probably in answer to Carl asking him who he thought he was. "Winslow is in a delicate position," Ty went on. "It's still his first day of heat, and he waited too long before getting help to make it through. He needs extra attention and care, and he does not need the stress of his deadbeat brother right now."

Carl shouted, "Who are you calling a deadbeat?" so loudly that I could hear it on the other end of the call.

I winced and silently held out my hand, the same way Ty had when he'd taken over the call earlier.

Ty eyed me for a moment, anger rippling off him...and making me ridiculously horny instead of terrified. Well, in addition to being terrified. But he also huffed a sigh, shook his head, and said into the phone, "Your brother wants to talk to you."

Ty handed the phone over. I sent him an apologetic look, then said, "Hey, Carl."

Carl didn't hesitate before launching into, "What sort of an asshole have you gotten yourself mixed up with? That guy is a total fucking jerk. You should get away from him right now and find someone else to deal with the rest of your heat. That guy sounds like he might hurt you."

"I can't go find someone else once my heat has already started," I said. Well, technically I could have, but having more than one alpha during heat was considered beyond gross.

At least, that's what they said. Honestly, I was getting to the level of horniness again where the thought of two alphas messing me up sounded pretty fucking good.

It helped nothing that those thoughts hit me as I stared at a glowering Ty. Maybe there was a way to clone him so that I could suck on his cock while he fucked into me so hard and deep that slick squirted everywhere, and—

"Carl, I've got to go," I said quickly, my voice hoarse with need.

I ended the call with Carl's voice ringing out in protest and threw my phone aside. I was only vaguely aware of my cock tenting the towel around my waist. I needed to wrap myself around Ty, and I needed it immediately.

Ty's expression changed from frustrated with Carl to sympathetic in a flash. "Is it another heat wave?" he asked.

"I think so," I said, wriggling as I felt slick start to seep out of my hole, which was throbbing and demanding to be filled. I was glad I had that towel under me. "I'm sorry about my brother," I said, sounding whinier than I wanted to. God, I hated not being able to control my body or my emotions. "He means well, he's just...." I didn't know how to finish the sentence.

"Never mind about your brother," Ty said, back to being the compassionate ESA he'd been so far. "Tell me what you need, baby."

A small frown pinched Ty's brow for a moment, but I almost didn't notice.

"I...." I squirmed where I sat, feeling like some kind of horny poltergeist had taken over my body and wanted me to do things that really weren't me.

"It's okay," Ty said, definitely professional again. He turned to me, moving one leg up onto the bed, and reached for my hand. "Heat makes omegas do things they wouldn't normally do. That's why I'm so angry with your brother for sending you out in such a vulnerable state. It doesn't mean there's anything wrong with you or that you're not a good person."

"I need to suck your cock," I blurted, then squeezed my eyes shut.

"Okay," Ty said calmly, as if I hadn't just made an ass of myself. "It's probably easiest if you kneel on the floor."

As he said that, he leaned back and reached for one of the pillows. Without so much as a blink, he dropped it to the floor at the foot of the bed, then scooted to the end of the bed, opening his legs wide.

I couldn't believe he would do that, and without hesitating or flinching. His dick stood out from his body, like some sort of missile ready to launch. His balls were pronounced, even though they were drawn up. Alpha anatomy was really something else.

"Whenever you're ready," Ty said in that soothing voice of his. "I'm here for you."

It was weird, but as awkward as I felt about the whole thing, a lot of the fear and hesitation I'd felt after that first time had melted away. Maybe that was what happened when you'd had someone's dick so far inside you that you could feel it in your heartbeat.

Still, I sent him one last look to make sure it was really okay, and when Ty nodded and smiled, I slipped off the bed, ditched the towel, and knelt on the pillow between his spread legs. And fuck, did it feel good to kneel for him. I wasn't particularly kinky, but kneeling in front of an alpha like that, knowing he could use me however he wanted to use me, was everything I'd never known I wanted and more.

In the end, it was the smile that did it. Ty was luminous when he smiled. He radiated warmth and security. His rainy forest scent was so strong as I rested my hands on his thighs and leaned into him that I was breathing it in with long, deep breaths, bringing my nose all the way to his balls, before I could stop myself. Not only that, I rubbed my cheeks against his groin, like some sort of slutty cat marking his owner with their scent, or being marked by Ty's.

Ty let out a grumbling sigh of pleasure and threaded his fingers loosely through my hair, and that was it for me. Slutty cat for the win.

With my eyes half-lidded with lust, I dragged my lips all the way up the long length of his cock, then kissed and licked the drops of moisture from his head. He was cut, which just seemed to increase my need to lick and suck and brush my lips over his flared head. There was something beyond the normal feeling that maybe the guy I was with would like what I was doing that I'd had when trying to blow someone before. It kind of felt like a paradox, but this was about me and what I needed.

Just playing with his tip and licking the pre-cum that formed wasn't enough for long. Even though it scared me a little because of Ty's size, I needed to take more of him. So I bore down, a little at a time, not entirely sure what to do with my tongue, but wanting as much of him as I could take.

I surprised myself by how enthusiastically I sucked him in until I gagged. I hated the gagging part of giving head, but now, with Ty's big, alpha cock almost to the back of my throat, it was like choking didn't matter. It was a vague thought in the back of my head. What took up every other brain cell I had was how fucking good he tasted and how right it felt for that cock to be inside of me as deeply as possible and in any way I could get it.

"That's right, sweetheart," Ty growled, stroking my head and massaging my scalp as I bobbed on him, sucking and swallowing and choking on instinct alone. "You're doing so good, so good."

I must have been, even though I didn't have a clue what I was doing, because Ty's voice was rough and his thighs were rock hard with tension under my hands.

"I know what you need, baby, and I'll give it to you," he went on, his voice more strangled than ever.

Speaking of strangled, I moaned and shook as I repeatedly took Ty so deep I couldn't breathe. All the while, I could feel my own orgasm building and building, and when Ty growled with pleasure and started to come down my throat, I started to come too.

It was everything my body needed. I couldn't stop myself from moaning between swallows, or digging my fingertips hard into Ty's thighs. Hormones and biology aside, it felt like I was swallowing liquid satisfaction with every spurt of Ty's orgasm. I could feel it coat my esophagus and work its way into my stomach. It felt like contentment filling me, and it was so, so good.

Even after Ty stopped coming, I didn't want to take his cock out of my mouth. My body felt weak, but also restless, after my own orgasm, but I just wanted to stay where I was, sucking on Ty's alpha cock like it was a pacifier. The fact that he didn't really soften, even after coming, was even better.

"Do you need more?" Ty asked me, winded. He stroked the back of my neck and my shoulders as I lay limp against him, my cheek pressed against the crease of his hip while just the head of his cock remained in my mouth.

I hadn't thought about it until he asked, but as soon as the question was past his lips, my hole throbbed, reminding me that it was where Ty's cock actually belonged.

I straightened, even though it was a challenge in my cock-drunk state, and released his dick with a wet pop. I looked plaintively up at him, sighing pitifully, even though I hated it, and said, "I need you in me."

Fortunately, Ty seemed to understand what I meant without me having to elaborate in humiliating detail.

"I've got you," he said, scooping me up under my arms as though I weighed nothing.

He reached for the bottle of spermicide while balancing me on his thighs with my knees on the bed. The bed looked a bit cluttered, with bottles and condoms and packs of wipes scattered everywhere, but I was beginning to see why having them all within arm's reach was a good thing.

"I'm not like this," I insisted, squirming on his lap as he opened the bottle of spermicide. "I swear, I'm not usually like this at all. I don't have time to be slutty like this. I have too many responsibilities. I have to take care of Carl, and as soon as this is all over, I have to find another job, and maybe another place to live, if I can't convince Mr. Caruthers to cut us some slack on the rent. I'm really not the type to—oh!"

My thoughts scrambled as Ty pressed a generous helping of the spermicide gel into my hole, then massaged it deeper with three fingers. Twenty-four hours ago, I would have said there was no way I could take three fingers from an alpha with hands as big as Ty's. Now I groaned and mewled and tried to fuck myself on those fingers with my head thrown back in lust.

"I get it," Ty said, a deep rumble in his voice. "It's normal for heat. Don't be too hard on yourself."

"You need to fuck me now," I growled, shifting and jerking against him, like my hole was seeking out his cock of its own accord. "I need it. I need you in me."

It was like the cycle began all over again, but at least this time, I knew more about what to expect. Ty was strong enough to lift me up and to bring me down right onto his hard dick. I let out an obscene sound of joy as he filled me. The way I sat on him sent his hot, thick spear straight through me, and as his head punched into my womb, I let out a wail that I was sure would disturb everyone on that floor of the hotel.

They could deal with it, as far as I was concerned. I grasped my hands around Ty's neck and rode his cock like there was no tomorrow. The man was a genius for thinking of that position, because it enabled me to use every bit of my strength and the leverage of the bed to fuck myself into oblivion.

I was vaguely aware of Ty's distinctly alpha groans and

more than a little swearing as he let me ride him. He braced himself on the bed with one hand and wrapped the other around my already pulsing cock, and that was it for me. I started coming and didn't stop as he fisted me, and as I bounced on him, shoving his cockhead deeper and deeper into my womb.

When the heat orgasm took over from the regular orgasm, I was pretty sure I saw God. My vision went completely white, and every cell in my body seemed to explode with pleasure. That was all I could think about, all I could feel. Nothing else mattered but the endless, throbbing waves of pleasure that pushed and pulled at my core and turned me inside out.

I think it must have gone on for about a hundred years, but when the bliss finally started to fade, Ty's knot was lodged heavily in my ass, stretching me almost to the point of pain, but I wouldn't have had it any other way. We were lying on the bed with me on top, so at some point he must have moved and pulled me with him. We were both sweaty and sticky with cum and slick, and I had my open mouth pressed against his neck, like some sort of vampire.

"You're back," Ty said, actually sounding cheerful.

I realized that he was stroking my back and ass with those big hands of his, and that I didn't want him to ever, ever stop.

I struggled to use my arms to support myself so that I could look down at him. He looked as messed up as I felt, but for some reason, that made me smile.

"Who would have thought that a scrawny little loser omega could wear a big, strong alpha like you out?" I asked, grinning down at him.

Ty's smile faltered, and he brushed a hand over my cheek, then pushed my sweat-damp hair back from my face. "You're not a loser, Winslow," he said, resting his hand on the side of my face.

My heart throbbed as if it were having its own orgasm. "In all fairness," I said, feeling way cockier than I should have right then, "you don't actually know me well enough to know if I'm a loser or not."

"You aren't," Ty said without hesitation. Then he smiled. "I'm a professional. I know these things."

I laughed. I shouldn't have. It was no laughing matter. Ty didn't know how badly I'd done in school, or how hard it was for me to keep a job—although I was willing to admit that was Carl's fault as much as mine, and keeping my grades up hadn't seemed as important as Mom dying of cancer. There was something about Ty that made those things so much less important than I usually thought they were.

In fact, the only thing that felt important as I lay sprawled across his broad, hairy chest, his knot fusing us together, every movement causing ripples of pleasure to sparkle through me, was Ty.

"Thank you for doing this for me," I said, resting my head on his shoulder and sighing. "I really don't know what would have happened to me if you hadn't found me this morning."

"I don't want to think about it," Ty said, circling his arms around me protectively, possessively. "I found you, and that's all that matters for the time being."

Until my heat was over. Those unspoken words loomed loud in my mind. I had three days max to enjoy this, to enjoy the pleasure of heat sex—any sex at all, since this was it for me—but more than that, to enjoy the feeling of someone taking care of me. It wasn't something I was going to take for granted, since it wasn't likely to happen ever again.

"These waves get easier after the first few times," I sighed, closing my eyes and feeling myself drifting off. "I feel like I know you better now than that first...."

I didn't finish my sentence. The thought escaped me

anyhow. I felt far too contented with my arms around my alpha, my hole stuffed with his knot, and my insides coated with his cum, to worry about anything else.

Chapter Six

Ty

I knew better. I one hundred percent knew better. But there were some things that you couldn't stop, whether you wanted to or not.

And I didn't want to stop.

"You have a little—" I gestured to the corner of Winslow's mouth as he chewed on the English muffin he'd just taken a huge bite out of, indicating the blob of strawberry jam.

"Huh?" Winslow blinked, pausing mid-chew. He touched his fingertips to the wrong corner of his mouth.

I knew better than to do it, but I leaned into him and licked the jam away, then kissed him—all of which was easy to do, since Winslow sat on my lap as we ate the huge breakfast I'd ordered for his second day of heat from the rolling table positioned at the foot of the bed.

Winslow laughed as I tried to coax him to open his mouth

for a deeper kiss. He chewed the rest of his bite, swallowed, then finally let me in to the sweet, sticky heat of his mouth.

"It's weird making out while eating," he mumbled with my tongue teasing him.

"Are you complaining, omega?" I demanded playfully.

"No," he said with a simple smile. Half a jammy English muffin still in his hand, he looped his arms over my shoulders and caved to my demand for a kiss.

I told myself that I'd relaxed protocol because Winslow was so inexperienced and because he'd been terrified when I'd found him yesterday. I justified the cuddling and kissing by telling myself it was my job as an ESA to adjust and adapt to the needs of my client, whatever they might be. I argued that Winslow deserved a break, since I now knew something about his home life, or what passed for it.

But I should have known better.

"Are you sure it's okay for me to eat so much when I'm about to hit the strongest heat waves of my entire heat?" Winslow asked, leaning back enough to look me in the eyes. "I'm not going to, you know, puke while you're fucking me in this next wave because I have a full stomach, am I?"

I grinned at the youthfulness of his question. Being twenty meant he wasn't really a kid anymore, but if the conversations we'd had in the last twenty-four hours were anything to go on, Winslow had had his adolescence cut short by his mom's illness and death, and because of that, he'd retained a lot of the markers of youth. Like uncertainty and a lack of self-confidence, and certain speech patterns.

"An English muffin and some bacon and eggs is hardly what I'd call stuffing yourself," I said, adjusting the way I held him as he went back to eating the English muffin in question. "And you need the nutrients."

"That's what those disgusting shakes are for," he said, glancing to the empty can on our breakfast table.

I chuckled and brushed my fingers through his hair. "They're not disgusting. They're scientifically formulated to provide all the essential nutrients that heat takes out of an omega."

"Ty, come on," Winslow said with a flat look. "They're gross. I mean, mango flavor? Who thought of that?"

"What flavor would you rather have, ba—" I nearly bit my tongue to stop the pet name. "Baby" and "Sweetheart" had been coming out of my mouth way too much in the last day, and it had to stop. I could justify the peculiarities of this particular heat call all I wanted, but if I kept saying things like that and snuggling with Winslow while we were knotted instead of making polite conversation, or allowing Winslow to silently gather his thoughts between waves, then I was in trouble.

And deep down, I knew I was already in trouble.

Serious trouble.

Winslow popped the last of his English muffin in his mouth and chewed it with a smile while studying my face. "You're really calm for an alpha, you know," he said with his mouth still full.

"Calm?" I blinked and shifted the way I held him.

He sat across my lap, like a baby, instead of astride my hips, like he had when he'd fucked himself on my cock so ferociously that we'd both lost it during one wave the afternoon before. I should have known when my alpha soul nearly took over entirely during that wave, as I came and came and came straight into his womb while roaring with possessive fervor that I'd crossed just about every line there was.

There had been nothing calm about that. Or about the way I'd pinned him, face down when a wave hit him in the middle of the night, and lifted his hips so I could fuck his pulsating hole with my tongue and lap up the sweet slick directly from his insides as he whimpered and wept and came over and over until I had to call housekeeping at two in the morning for a new set of sheets.

The third set we'd gone through since his heat started.

"Yeah, calm," Winslow said with a shrug. He wiped his hands on the hotel robe thrown loosely around his shoulders —though it was completely open in the front, hiding nothing —then squirmed and wriggled and climbed around until he was straddling me. "I always thought alphas go ape-shit when they're around omegas in heat, but you've done a really good job of keeping it together."

I growled like a feral creature who wanted to tear his ass wide open as his groin slipped into close contact with mine.

Winslow laughed, and the sound had me so hard it was borderline painful. "Yeah, like that," he said, looping his arms around my shoulders again.

I hadn't been joking with him. My sweet omega had no idea that my control was hanging on by a thread.

And that control *had* to hang on. It absolutely, one hundred percent had to.

"I'm a professional," I said. My voice came out sounding like the Big Bad Wolf.

"I can tell," Winslow said. He wriggled like he was trying to get comfortable.

Those movements had my heart racing and my cock throbbing. I was surprised Winslow didn't say anything—like, "My Grandmama, what a big, hard, dripping cock you have" —but since I'd been almost constantly hard since we'd first tumbled into bed the morning before, he probably thought it was normal for an alpha with an omega in heat.

It absolutely was not normal.

Usually, as soon as my knot went down when I was with an ordinary client, I would go flaccid until the omega's next wave started.

With Winslow, I'd been hard so much of the time that part of me was beginning to wonder if it was a danger to my health. It wasn't. I had enough training and knew enough about alpha physiology to know that my body's extreme reaction fell within the bounds of normal.

With one tiny little caveat.

"I have to pee," Winslow said, wriggling off me and shedding his robe. "I'll be right back. I think I'm about to hit another wave anyhow."

He peeled away, then hesitated. A glimmer filled his bright, blue eyes, then he rushed in and gave me a quick peck on the lips before scurrying off to the bathroom.

It was the sweetest fucking thing anyone had ever done to me.

And as I watched Winslow's pert, round ass, its crease shiny with slick, walk away from me, I felt the whisper of an imaginary cord between us stretch.

"No," I warned myself once the bathroom door shut and Winslow couldn't hear me. "Absolutely not. No."

I stood and pushed the rolling table back, tidying up the remaining breakfast things as I did. I had to focus, to concentrate on getting the job done as professionally as possible. Now was not the time to get sentimental and to start believing in things like bonding at first sight. After twenty years of marriage, yes, but not after twenty-four hours of heat with an omega I didn't know from Adam the day before yesterday.

But there it was, that glittering filament of connection, that softness in my core that enabled me to feel how relaxed and happy Winslow was and how much he was looking forward to this next wave. It was a one-eighty from the fear he'd felt when I'd found him, but like he'd said, that was because I had a carefully cultivated calming presence, not because his omega instinctively trusted my alpha.

Ten years. I sighed heavily and rolled the table to the hotel room door. I peeked through the eyehole to make certain no one was in the hall, then I quickly opened the door and rolled the table to the hall, showing as little of my naked self to anyone who might be looking out through their own doors as possible. I'd been Bangers & Mash's best ESA for ten years, never having a complaint, never letting an omega down...and now this.

I shut the door and leaned against it, listening to the sound of the shower running in the bathroom. I was glad Winslow had decided to take a quick shower before his next wave. I needed the break to gather my thoughts.

I rubbed my hands over my stubbly face, resting my head back. How had I walked into this situation without seeing it coming? I'd had hundreds of clients in my career as an ESA, and not once had I come even close to bonding with any of them. I prided myself on that fact. My track record was what gave anxious omegas in need of help the confidence to hire me for their heats.

Contrary to what some old-fashioned people liked to think, omegas didn't necessarily want to bond with the alpha who took them through heat. These days, most unattached omegas wanted to get through the inconvenience of heat in the safest and most pleasurable way possible, then move on with their lives without attachments. I knew that, and I felt like it was my purpose in life to serve omegas that way.

Bonding with a client was a disaster. Bonding with someone who wasn't even a client, who was a mistake I'd made in a moment of misguided altruism, was even worse. I had a career to think of. Salazar Banger and Nicholas Mash relied on me. I hadn't worked my way up to the top tier of the company by falling for my clients.

I let out a breath and pushed away from the door, shocked

by where my thoughts had gone. *Falling* for a client? That was worse than just bonding with them.

Although one didn't generally happen without the other.

And Winslow wasn't just a client.

I paced around the hotel room as I listened to the shower, shoving my hands through my hair and rubbing my face. I had plans for the future, plans to help B&M go national. Yes, I could take a desk job, one that didn't involve servicing clients, but would that be enough to fulfill me? I loved that part of the job—not because it meant I could have blazing hot heat sex a couple times a month, but because nothing could replace the feeling I got when an anxious and stressed omega relaxed and put their trust in me to see them through a vulnerable time. Sure, it had just been a job when I'd first applied and gone through training, but after those first couple of clients, just seeing how much of a difference an ESA could make, I'd known I'd found my calling.

The sound of the shower stopped, and was followed by the scrape of a shower curtain being pulled back. Winslow's tread was too light for me to hear him getting out of the shower, but I could imagine him grabbing a fluffy, white towel and rubbing it all over that slight, lean body of his.

I groaned at the mental image as my dick twitched, and marched back to the bed to straighten up. I took a few deep breaths to try to push the connected feeling away. Yes, it felt good. Sure, it felt natural and right, like all of the odd pieces of my life had suddenly come together and brought stunning clarity with them. But it wasn't what I wanted. I had a career. People were counting on me. I needed to snap out of it and snap the bond that—

"I hope you don't mind that I took a shower."

Winslow's voice washed over me like the sound of waves breaking against the shore on those childhood beach days. His lollipop scent flew at me like a sea breeze, freezing me as I leaned over the bed, lining up the bottles of lube and spermicide, and a packet of wipes. I had a strip of condoms that had fallen out of the box in my hand too, and as Winslow's scent enveloped me, the alpha in me wanted to throw the condoms and the remaining spermicide out the window.

Ironically, that snapped me back to my senses. I stood straight and turned to Winslow, managing a genuine smile for how fresh and inviting he looked. I could contemplate bonding and affection all I wanted, but I absolutely drew the line at impregnating an omega without his or her expressed permission, and without discussing it at length first.

"If showering makes you feel better, then I am all for it," I said, setting the condoms aside, then taking a step toward Winslow.

"It's weird," he said, walking slowly to me, scrubbing a hand through his wet hair as he did. "I'm kind of a bit of a clean freak when it comes to personal hygiene, but something inside me kept telling me not to wash all the slick and spunk and sweat off. Is that normal?"

I caught my breath. The way Winslow kept asking me if the most ordinary things were normal was ridiculously endearing. So was the bright, eager look in his eyes and the pink flush of his skin. He'd been shy about his body with me yesterday, but now he walked right up to me and rested his hands on my chest without seeming to give it a second thought, even though his dick was already half-hard in the build-up to the next wave.

"It's perfectly normal, baby," I said, then kissed his forehead.

Fuck's sake! I had to stop.

Except, I couldn't. Deep down, I knew that. It was already too late.

"Remember what we talked about last night?" I said

instead, faking the calm that he thought I had as I took his hand, then drew him to sit on the bed with me.

"Alpha ejaculate is loaded with chemicals and hormones that are absorbed through an omega's skin and membranes to cause a sense of pleasure and satisfaction and to make an omega feel more open to their alpha partner," Winslow repeated the lesson I'd given him last night between waves, as we'd eaten a small supper.

I moved to sit with my back against the headboard, thinking it wouldn't leave enough room for Winslow to do more than sit beside me.

I was wrong.

Winslow practically crawled up my body, siting astride my hips again, even though it meant his knees were wedged against the padded headboard, and bringing our cocks and balls into direct contact.

Even with that boldly sexual move, Winslow continued to speak as though we were in a study session before a test and not teetering on the verge of a peak heat wave.

"The intensity of the urges and emotions that both alphas and omegas feel during heat are Nature's way of encouraging breeding and reproduction."

Winslow paused and tilted his head to one side. His hands continued to rove my body, almost as if they had a mind of their own, making it hard for me to sit still.

"I've never really thought about reproducing," he said, focusing on me again, though his pupils were getting wider with each passing second. "I kind of do want to have kids someday, but I don't know if it will ever be possible. The way things are now, me having a baby would be an absolute catastrophe."

"That's why Bangers & Mash was founded," I said, proud of myself for not adding, "sweetheart" to the end of my sentence, even though the urge was there. "The founders are definitely family men. They have three kids themselves. I'm good friends with one of them; Phillip is his name. But they understand that just because our biology tells us we should be reproducing like rabbits, that doesn't mean it's actually the right thing to do. We'll have children when we're ready."

Winslow froze, blinking at me. I was stunned by those words myself. I hadn't expected them at all. I wanted to snatch them back—or maybe not—and I wanted to brush them off—possibly—and pretend I'd never said them. This was not what I needed, not what I wanted at all. I didn't know Winslow. Yes, we'd talked a lot in the first day of his heat and we'd shared mind-bending pleasure, but we'd just met. He'd told me things about his life, but I hadn't returned that favor, not really, other than to tell him how much I loved my job.

Bonding was for long-time married couples.

Fated mates were a flat-out fairy tale.

"I meant, each of us having our own children someday," I stammered, definitely not feeling like a professional with ten years of experience. "Not the two of us together."

The tight laugh that escaped from me as I said that was as bad as an admission of guilt.

"No, of course not." Winslow laughed as well, the same guilty "I wouldn't dream of that, except that's exactly what I was dreaming of" laugh. "And besides, you've got way better things to do than getting involved with me and Carl and our shitty lives."

"I don't have anything better to do," I said too fast, cradling Winslow's face with one hand. I winced, closed my eyes for a second, and went on with, "I mean, your life is not shitty. You've just been dealt a rough hand early on in life. Being with an omega in heat gives you insight into their character—" and now I was lying, or twisting the truth, since that only applied if there was a bond, "—and I just know that you're smart and tough, and that you're going to do brilliant things with your life."

Winslow laughed and pressed his cheek into my palm, eyes downcast. "Part of me wants to say that's a lot of wishful thinking." He met my eyes again, his pupils even wider and his skin more flushed. "The rest of me wants to make a joke that the only brilliant thing I want to do is you. It's happening again. Oh, God, this one is going to be strong. I need you in me, Ty. Wow, this one is hitting me hard and fast, just like I want you to hit my womb."

He laughed, then wriggled against me, suddenly breathless and restless.

"Okay, that was bad, but this one is really strong," he finished, then started whimpering.

"I know, baby, I know," I said, pulling him in for a kiss.

Fuck the ethics of calling a client by a pet name. Winslow was right when he said this wave was going to be strong. I could smell it and feel it, and my alpha was already roaring in response.

I flipped Winslow so that he was facing away from me, then pushed his head and shoulders down so I could fuck him from behind. The position would give me the greatest amount of control and allow me to thrust as hard and deep as I could, as hard and deep as he would need me to.

"You're hitting the peak of your heat," I explained in a vain attempt to remain detached and academic about it as I reached for the spermicide.

Technically, I should be using a condom during his peak, since that's when impregnation was most likely, but my alpha demanded to feel Winslow's insides directly. I needed to come straight into my omega's womb, for both of our sakes.

"It will get easier from here," I told him as I washed his hole with the spermicide, then pushed into him.

Winslow gasped with pleasure, and his body vibrated as he

started to come. I let out a thunderous sound of passion to match his as I curled over his sinewy body and started to pound him with the most powerful need I'd ever felt.

It would not get easier from here. It would definitely get better and give us both more pleasure, but the direction we were heading in would definitely not make things easier on either of us.

Chapter Seven

Winslow

After three solid days of fucking, I felt like I'd been beat up. Mostly on the inside. I had a persistent sensation of soreness and fullness in my abdomen, and my throat was as raw as if I were coming down with a cold. Part of me just hoped Ty's cockhead felt equally sore from all the punching.

I laughed vaguely at that little joke as I lay on my stomach, still a little bit asleep, early in the morning of the fourth day since my heat started. Everything had changed. I felt it as soon as I woke up, but a huge chunk of my brain was still in denial about it. I wasn't horny anymore, for one thing. Heat-horny was an emotion I wouldn't soon forget, but it was gone now.

A different feeling replaced that overwhelming need to be fucked into oblivion—satisfaction. Not just physical satisfaction—like I'd been fucked so good and hard and filled with alpha cum to the point where it was probably flowing through my veins instead of blood—but also the satisfaction that came with a job well done. Like my body was telling my mind, "Well done, buddy," and the two of them were toasting to their success and resting on their laurels.

As nice as that sensation was, my heart hadn't been invited to the party. Something wasn't quite right there. As blissed out as my body felt as I woke up fully and rubbed my face against the pillow to clear my head, something deep within me was sad.

It was over. Three mind-blowing days of heat sex with a gorgeous, kind, interesting alpha who had taken my virginity in the absolute best way possible. I couldn't believe it.

I rolled to my side, blinked, and breathed for a moment, then pushed myself a little more to sit. My body definitely felt like I'd been beat with baseball bats, and had one shoved repeatedly up my ass and down my throat. I groaned and stretched, trying to rid myself of the feeling, but mostly aware of the gaping hole even deeper inside of me where Ty should have been.

The shower was running in the bathroom, so I knew where he was. It was the weirdest thing, but I had this inner sense that he was feeling blue too. I could practically see the frown on his face as he fought off inconvenient emotion and reminded himself he was an alpha and a professional so he shouldn't get sad.

That actually made me smile a bit as I threw back the bedcovers and tested what kind of shape my body was in by climbing out of bed. I shouldn't feel like I knew Ty so well after only three days, but I supposed when you spent three days literally joined with someone else, you got to know them really fast.

As I stood, thick liquid oozed from my ass. The sensation immediately had me flushing hot and scrambling for one of the towels that had been thrown over the back of a chair at some point the day before. I guessed all that cum and leftover slick I thought was running through my veins now was actually running somewhere else. High school Health class hadn't covered what happens when all those bodily fluids that had ended up inside you during heat made their way out. They hadn't covered a lot of things in school.

I grabbed the towel as fast as I could, trickles of spunk running down the backs of my thighs, and threw it on the foot of the bed, then sat. Even though I was alone in the room—the shower shut off just as I sat—it was mortifying to...leak like that.

I didn't do anything but sit on the towel, wondering if I should get another one, and feeling that sense of sadness swell within me as I listened to Ty shuffle in the bathroom. I needed a shower in the worst way, but it was the sounds and sense of Ty's presence that occupied most of my thoughts, right up until the moment he opened the bathroom door and stepped back into the room.

"You're up," he said with a warm smile that went straight to my core.

Ty had a towel around his waist, but his torso was still bare and gorgeous. My body tingled with the memory of what his skin and chest hair felt like stretched along my body, hot and sweaty and masterful. His smile made me feel like I might actually be valuable in some way.

And then he walked closer to me, reaching out like he would cup my face or ruffle my already disastrous hair, and I gasped and scrambled away from him.

The reaction came out of nowhere, and it was overpowering. My embarrassment over leaking heat juice out my ass was forgotten as I hurried to put space between us. My heart pounded like I was in danger.

"Oh my God, I'm sorry," I said as soon as I realized what I'd done. I forced myself to stop and stand where I was, meeting Ty's eyes sheepishly. "I'm not scared of you, I swear. I don't know what came over me just now. I really like you."

I took a step forward, intending to maybe hug him to prove it, but a sudden sense of revulsion swept through me, and I pulled my arms back with a grimace.

Ty's cheerful smile dropped, and for a moment, I felt a powerful wave of grief radiate from him.

A moment after that, he schooled his expression into professional calm. "Don't worry," he said. "It's perfectly normal. Your heat has ended, and for the first few hours after it ends, omegas feel compelled to get as far away from alphas as possible. Even their mates—er, if they have mates," he rushed to add.

I wasn't sure why he needed to add that...except that it made me feel better about the reaction I had to him specifically.

"How long does it usually last?" I asked, hugging myself and glancing past Ty's shoulder to the bathroom. God, I needed a shower.

Almost as if Ty had heard that thought, he said, "It can last up to a day. It all depends on how much—" he cleared his throat, "—ejaculate you have left in your body. If you take a shower and rinse some of it out, the feelings of aversion should lessen. By the end of the day, you should be clear enough that things will be back to normal."

I nodded silently at him, feeling young and stupid, especially in relation to him. Ty was older and wiser, and he was definitely more experienced. He knew things. He had a career, not just a job, and was important and respected. I was just some dumb kid who had been fired from a crap job the day before he'd found me out of my mind with my first heat. He was so out of my league.

And yet, as I said, "Okay, then, I'll just go take a shower," and moved past him, a knot of panic formed in my gut over the prospect of leaving him. I didn't think I could stand him touching me right then, but I also couldn't stand the thought of walking out of Ty's life and never seeing him again either.

And that wasn't an exaggeration at all. As I stepped into a blissfully hot shower a couple minutes later and stuck my head under the spray, a sob escaped me, and I started crying despite every effort I made to stop. It was wild and weird, but thinking about Ty leaving—which was all I could think about as I turned my ass to the shower spray, then used the convenient nozzle attachment to clean my sore and tender insides out— made me feel like my heart was crumbling and I would never be whole again.

I finished up the shower with a thorough scrub, using the hotel's nice-smelling soap and shampoo, but as I turned off the water and stepped out to dry myself off, I couldn't remember a time when I'd been so depressed. It was almost as bad as those final weeks of Mom's life, when I'd sat by her bedside, holding her hand, and listening to her breathing turn into that death-rattle that made the hair on the back of my neck stand up.

I shook my head to get rid of the images that came with the memory of Mom, and closed my eyes, forcing myself to remember her smiling face from when I was a kid, before she got sick. That helped with the Mom aspect of my grief, but not with the Ty part of it. I took a few deep breaths, brushed my teeth, combed my hair, and when I was satisfied I could handle it, I headed out of the bathroom with a towel around my waist.

Ty was dressed, the bed was slightly neater than when I'd left it, and he'd laid out my clothes—which he'd sent to the hotel laundry when I was sleeping on that second day of heat. He must have ordered breakfast when I was in the shower too, because the rolling table was back, and it was piled high with food. As I took a few, tentative steps toward the bed, Ty glanced up from where he'd been repacking what was left of the heat kit he'd brought with him and smiled at me.

I lost it. It was so embarrassing. I started crying like a baby, even though it didn't make sense to me.

Ty dropped everything and headed toward me. "Hey, hey, it's okay, ba—"

I cried even harder when Ty stopped himself from calling me baby.

I wanted him to hug me and hold me and never let me go, but when he came within a hair's breadth of doing just that, I gasped and jumped away from him.

That only made me cry harder as I sagged with my back against the wall.

"What's wrong with me?" I wailed. "This is stupid. I don't cry like this. It's like the emotions are coming from outside of me."

"Yep," Ty said, nodding, but also frowning. "That's normal too. Your hormones went a little crazy during heat, and it'll take a while for them to stabilize."

"How long?" I demanded, angry now. "Because this sucks balls."

Ty's beautiful mouth curved into a smile. "It depends on a lot of things. Omega hormones regulate again in anywhere from a day to a week."

"A week?" I burst into tears again. "I cannot handle this for a week."

"It's okay," Ty said, inching closer to me, but wavering, as if he were fighting some sort of instinct too.

"Is it normal that I simultaneously need you to hold me and that I can't stand the idea of you touching me at the same time?" I asked, lifting my stinging eyes to him. "Like, I need your arms around me or I think I might die, but if you touch me, I know it will burn like acid."

I expected the same sort of clinical, ESA answer he'd given me at the start when he explained things, but instead, Ty blew out a frustrated breath and rubbed a hand over his face. He hadn't shaved in three days, and a slight beard now covered his chin and jaw. I still felt the effects of that beard all along my inner thighs.

The sense I had that something was really wrong increased when he said, "Winslow, we need to talk."

I swallowed, then followed him to the bed when he gestured for me to move. That was another thing. I needed to do what Ty said on a visceral level. Yeah, I was a people-pleaser at heart—another omega trait that was stupidly cliché, but I had it—but it was ten times more potent when Ty wanted me to do something.

Before sitting on the foot of the bed, I reached for my clothes. As Ty pulled the breakfast table close to the bed, I quickly ditched the towel and dressed in my jeans and t-shirt. That was enough for the time being. I sat, feeling way too much like a kid who had been called to the principal's office, and Ty sort of trapped me against the bed by wheeling the table right up in front of me.

He sat, keeping a comfortable distance between us, and reached for the coffee pot. As he poured for both of us, he said, "We need to talk about what's happened."

"What's happened?" I asked, a little worried Carl had called while I'd been out of it and there was yet another disaster at home.

Ty frowned, like he was having trouble putting his thoughts into words, and handed me a mug of coffee. Our fingers brushed slightly, which felt like I'd stuck my whole hand in an electrical socket.

"That," Ty said.

I blinked at him. "What do you mean?" I asked, reaching for the cream and sugar.

"That spark when I handed you your coffee. That's not normal."

I swallowed a gulp of coffee black, worried that I would need something harsh and bitter to help slap sense into me as Ty told me whatever he had to tell me. It was bad news, I knew. I was probably dying. He'd probably fucked me so hard he ruptured something, and the fluid that had spilled out of me—and I could still feel a little more of it now, which wasn't great news for my jeans—meant I was dying.

Instead, Ty seemed to summon his courage and say, "I'm almost one hundred percent certain that we bonded during your heat."

I held my breath, freezing midway through adding cream and sugar to my coffee, since I couldn't handle it black after all, and blinked at him.

"That's not possible...is it?" I asked, moving again. "People only bond after they've been together for ages. It doesn't happen with complete strangers."

Even as I said it, I felt like I was hurling a horrible insult at Ty by calling him a complete stranger. He wasn't. I could feel it in my core, in my dick, and in my heart. We might have only met a few days ago, and under weird circumstances, but every cell in my body screamed that Ty was not a stranger, he was—

Oh, God. We'd bonded.

"These things happen sometimes," Ty said after taking a long gulp of coffee. "It happened to a friend of mine, actually. It's extraordinarily rare. But I can feel it, and I suspect you can too."

I looked at him over the lip of my coffee mug as I gulped some of the much-needed caffeine. Bonded. To a gorgeous, important alpha who had his shit together. Me.

But yeah, I *could* feel it. I could feel the sense of peace and belonging that sitting near him gave me. I couldn't read his mind, but I had a strong sense of his emotions. He was confused and frustrated, and a little bit happy and pleased with himself in that macho way alphas had underneath all that.

"Honestly, I'm not sure what happens next," Ty went on before I could summon up the brain cells to say anything. "Bonds don't just form and break randomly. This isn't the sort of thing we'll get over if we go our separate ways and forget about it. In fact," he paused to wince, then reached for the plastic wrap covering the breakfast plate in front of me, like he was my alpha and he needed to provide for me—which might be an actual thing now—then said, "I think we might need to stay close for a while."

He balled up the plastic wrap and threw it on the table with a huff, then handed me a fork. He nodded for me to eat, then said, "I don't know how this is going to work. I have a business trip to Norwalk the day after tomorrow, and...and I guess you have to come with me. Bonds aren't always like this, but when they first form, especially if they form suddenly, during a heat...." He didn't finish his sentence. Instead, he shook his head and muttered something under his breath.

I had tried to do as he ordered again by eating as he spoke, but I nearly choked when the full impact of what he was saying hit me.

"Oh, God," I gulped some coffee to wash down the bite of pancakes. "I've ruined everything, haven't I? You're an ESA. It's your job to fuck omegas."

"I don't think of it like that," he said as if trying to placate me.

It didn't work. My eyes went wider, and my stomach twisted. Mostly because the thought of Ty fucking, or even touching, another omega brought me really close to puking. Like, for real, not just metaphorically.

"You can't keep being an ESA if you're bonded," I nearly

shouted. I meant it to be a statement of fact, but it came out sounding like I was making a demand.

"The thought has crossed my mind, yes," Ty said with brittle calm.

I gaped at him even more. What had he told me during our pillow-talk between heat waves? "You've been doing this for ten years. I just obliterated your ten-year career. I've ruined everything."

I threw my fork down, trying to push the table back and stand.

"Hey, hey," Ty spoke calmly. He reached for my wrist to keep me from fleeing.

The touch felt like fire, but it also felt right. I sat down again so fast I nearly spilled backwards.

"We'll figure this out," Ty said, sounding more alpha than ever. "Eat your breakfast. You need the nutrients. You're depleted in several different ways right now, which also means you're not thinking clearly. Nothing has to be solved right now."

I let out a breath. He was right about that. I picked up my fork and used the edge to carve out another piece of pancake—not because he'd compelled me to or anything, but because his words had made me realize how fucking hungry I was.

"We'll figure this out," Ty repeated. "Half the people I work with at B&M are married. I'm sure there will be options."

I glanced sideways at him as I chewed, wondering if that were true and if he believed it.

We ate breakfast in silence, both of us lost in our thoughts. I was such a loser. My very first heat, my first ever sexual partner, and I'd exploded a life he'd spent ten years building. He didn't deserve the curse of me. And I was sure that was what he was thinking too, based on his frown as he ate.

Except, what I felt from him was more like resolution and

determination. A lot of uncertainty too, but definitely calm, and when he glanced to me a few times, I felt a burst of affection, like the gooey, sweet center of a candy bursting out when you bit into it.

After breakfast, we tidied up the room as best we could, although Ty explained that the hotel staff was used to cleaning up after heat calls and I shouldn't be embarrassed by what we left behind. Which, of course, made me think about it and get embarrassed.

"I don't know how to handle everything about the situation we're now in," Ty said as we rode the elevator down to the parking garage, "but let's just take one step at a time. I'll drive you home first and we can assess the situation there."

I wasn't sure what he was talking about. I climbed into his big, shiny truck once we reached the garage, then gave him directions to the not-so-great part of town once we were out on the road. We managed to chat about the weather a bit, and I explained a little about how Carl and I had found the apartment when we were both so young.

I was just telling Ty how generous Mr. Caruthers, our landlord, had been with us as we pulled up to the apartment... and found Mr. Caruthers himself throwing my and Carl's suitcases out the front door and into the yard, where several boxes of our belongings were already scattered around.

"No!" I gasped, fumbling with the handle of the truck's door as Ty parked on one of the empty spots out front. "No, no, no! He's been threatening us, but I didn't think he'd actually do it."

"Do what?" Ty asked as I managed to push the door open.

I glanced over his shoulder to him and said, "Evict us."

Chapter Eight

Ty

Winslow wasn't the only one reeling from the inescapable fact of our bond. And I knew he was reeling. I could feel it. I was having a hard time wrapping my head around the whole thing myself. It had been easy to brush the reality of bonding with an omega aside in the middle of his heat—blisteringly hot heat sex with a bonded mate had a way of doing that—but once Winslow hit the post-heat aversion to touch, it brought everything into too-sharp focus.

I was responsible for a stranger. A stranger who wasn't really a stranger. It was like I'd read the cheat-sheet of Winslow's heart and soul and had skipped straight to the point where it felt like I'd known him for years. Really felt it, in every cell of my body. The important part was that I felt a visceral need to take care of him, the same way I had an inherent need to take care of myself. And from the moment I pulled the Ranger into a parking space and saw the middle-aged beta throwing suitcases out onto the weed-filled yard in front of a run-down apartment building, the alpha in me roared.

"He swore he wouldn't do it," Winslow muttered in a panic as he slipped out of the truck. "He said he'd give us more time."

I put a few pieces together as I cut the engine and got out of the truck to follow my omega—there was no point in stopping myself from thinking those words now—as he cut across the uneven lawn to the path leading up to the apartment building door. Winslow had briefly mentioned something about not having any money to pay him or to pay the rent. His brother, Carl—who must have been the lanky beta scrambling around the yard, picking up bits and pieces while hurling curse words and insults at the landlord—had said there might be trouble.

Carl hadn't called in the last two days. At least, not that I knew of. He'd either respected the fact that Winslow was in heat, or he'd been too busy doing whatever had happened to cause the landlord to evict him and Winslow after, apparently, promising he wouldn't.

"Winslow!" Carl shouted, dropping everything in his arms as he noticed Winslow approaching from the parking lot. "Thank God you're here. Is it over? Is your heat finished?" He glanced in my direction, then asked, "Is that the alphahole who chewed me out over the phone the other day?"

I balled my hands into fists to keep from pummeling the mouthy beta right then and there. How dare he blurt out questions about Winslow's heat in public, when some of their neighbors were looking on? While talking about heat didn't carry the same sort of stigma that it once had, it was still considered gauche. Did Carl have no respect for his sensitive, beautiful, tough brother at all?

The answer to that was crystal clear when Carl dashed

forward, heedless of how Winslow was feeling post-heat, and grabbed his arm to drag him onto the path, saying, "You have to talk to Mr. Caruthers. See if you can work your magic to stop him from throwing us out."

I didn't just see the wince that pinched Winslow's face, I felt his burst of discomfort at his brother's touch. It would have been worse if I'd touched him, but omegas were averse to anyone touching them in the first few hours after their heat ended, not just their alphas.

Winslow shook out of Carl's grip, glancing around forlornly at the boxes and random items scattered all over the yard, then sighed. "Let me see what I can do," he said, turning to march up the path to the building's front door.

I wasn't about to let Winslow face this alone. I strode up to his side, glaring briefly at Carl as I did. By the time I reached Winslow, he was just about to step onto the small, concrete porch that made up the shabby building's entrance.

We were stopped as the landlord, Mr. Caruthers, appeared in the door again with a full trash bag of what I assumed was more of Winslow's and Carl's things.

"Where the fuck have you been?" Mr. Caruthers asked with an ominous frown.

"I can explain," Winslow said, holding up his hands.

I stepped forward, glaring at the landlord. "What the hell is going on here?" I demanded. It was probably taking things too far to put so much aggression into my tone, particularly since the landlord was a beta and not another alpha, but I was in full protective mode.

The landlord flinched and took a step back, then seemed to regroup and overcome his initial reaction to my alphaness.

"Do you know these boys?" he asked.

"I do." I nodded, resting a hand on Winslow's shoulder in order to send the subtle message that he was mine.

Of course, I had to take it away again when Winslow reacted like I'd burned him.

The landlord glanced between us, seeming to get the gist of things anyhow—which was another sign of the bond. If other people, betas, were picking up on it, it must have been strong.

"They're two months behind on their rent," the landlord said.

"*Two* months?" Winslow gaped, then pivoted to glare at his brother.

"I'm not running a charity here," the landlord went on. "I was willing to let it slide for one month, but two? And then I heard that this one lost his job the other day."

Winslow turned around all the way and stepped down from the porch. "What happened to the rent money, Carl? I gave it to you to pay Mr. Caruthers."

Carl laughed anxiously and rolled his shoulders, like he knew he'd been nailed. "I invested it," he said. "You know James from the mini-mart? He let me in on this great website he's a part of. You can buy just about anything there, and what you do is send your link to people so they can go online and buy stuff using your code. And they get a code too, so whenever you get a referral through them, it doubles your amount of commission."

"You gave up our rent money for a pyramid scheme?" Winslow pulsed with anger as he approached his brother. I could feel it as if he were radiating heat like a furnace.

"The kid is dumb," the landlord said to me, narrowing his eyes at Carl. "This isn't the first stupid idea he's had. If not for Winslow, I would have kicked him out ages ago." He paused, then added in a regretful tone, "Winslow's a good egg, but enough is enough."

I resented the way the landlord spoke to me like we were on the same side, but I had other things to deal with.

"Carl, how many times have I told you that those things are scams?" Winslow asked, sounding exhausted, as he stopped in front of his brother. He crossed his arms tightly and frowned. "There is no such thing as a get rich quick scheme. You can't keep *investing* our rent money in these things."

"That vending machine at the mall was a good idea," Carl argued.

"Yeah, until you stopped stocking it," Winslow said, sounding more gloomy than angry.

"I couldn't afford to buy more stock. I needed the money from the machine to buy you that bicycle," Carl argued. "Can you imagine what would have happened if you hadn't had that bicycle?"

I felt a wave of guilt and frustration from Winslow that had me balling my hands into fists again.

As I stepped down from the porch and marched to Winslow's side, Winslow said, "You sold the bike last week, and God only knows why. They fired me from the café because I was late too many times and showed up sweaty and stinking from trying to run to work to get there in time."

I breathed in instinctively at Winslow's mention of scent. He still smelled like the lollipops of my childhood, but now that his heat had passed, it was more like a light perfume and not an overpowering deluge. But if he'd been showing up to work with a strong scent after running to get there, I was willing to bet that it wasn't the sweat stink that had gotten him fired, it was probably the omega scent causing havoc with café customers.

"I'll make it up to you," Carl said, moving quickly to pick up some of their things from the grass. "I swear, I'll make it up to you. I heard about this thing where I can go door to door selling knives, just like people used to back in the day. Apparently, it's really—"

"You aren't going to do anything like that," I cut Carl off.

Carl straightened, dropping the things he'd just picked up, and glared at me. "You don't have anything to do with this, *alpha*," he snapped, as if "alpha" were an insult. "Who are you anyhow? You don't know us. You're just some...some sex worker who picked my brother up for some fun when he went into heat."

The neighbors who were watching the scene from a second-floor balcony gasped. The landlord looked surprised, and a little embarrassed over the way Carl had just blurted it out.

"I bet you didn't even pay him for the pleasure, did you?" Carl went on, evidently not realizing he'd already pushed his luck past its limits. When he repeated, "Did you?" with a hopeful look, I was done.

I closed the gap between us and grabbed the front of his shirt, lifting him to his toes. "You will not now, nor ever again, disrespect your brother, in public or in private. Do you understand?"

"I—I—uh—um—" Carl sputtered, totally taken by surprise.

"Ty, don't," Winslow said quietly behind me. I could feel the humiliation spilling off him. "He doesn't mean any harm. He never means any harm."

Out of respect for Winslow, and that alone, I let Carl go. I wasn't usually like this. I'd always considered myself more of the gentle giant type, not an intimidating thug. I knew better than to let the heat hormones scramble my brain like this.

I took a step back, forcing myself to breathe and get a grip. Winslow had a big, immediate problem, and it wasn't Carl. Carl was more of a persistent, nagging itch.

I turned back to the landlord, glancing to Winslow first. "I'll take care of this," I said with certainty and authority.

"Okay," Winslow said, taking a half step back. That, I liked. What I didn't like was the way my omega curled in on himself, shrinking, as if he'd been the one to do something wrong.

"None of this is your fault, sweetheart," I said, not even caring I'd used a pet name with Carl, the landlord, and the neighbors looking on.

Carl let out a low, "Ohh," but I ignored that too.

I stepped back onto the porch and squared my shoulders as I faced the landlord.

"What's the actual situation here?" I asked. "Can we come to some sort of an agreement?"

The landlord sighed and shoved a hand through his balding hair. He looked at Winslow with regret for a moment, then frowned as he watched Carl attempt to pick things up from the yard again. "I've already rented their apartment to someone else," he said. "The new tenant signed the lease yesterday. What's done is done."

I growled, mostly in thought, but the sound seemed to rattle the landlord.

"I could push back the move-in date by a week," he said quickly. "That would give Winslow and Carl more time to clear out their things, and I'd still have a few days to clean and repaint the place."

Not only did I have the sense that was the best deal we were going to get, I didn't want my omega living in that sad building with those nosy neighbors for another second anyhow.

I was inches away from making the deal myself, but I managed to turn to Winslow to ask, "Is that alright with you?" We might have been bonded, but I was determined not to be one of those alphas that kept their omega more like a pet than a partner.

Winslow sighed and glanced around at his things in the yard, and at Carl picking them up—and getting distracted—then back at me. He shrugged and said, "We don't have anywhere else to live. I've tried to look before, but we don't have money for a deposit and...." He sent a guilty look to Carl, who wasn't paying attention, then stepped closer to me and lowered his voice. "And none of the good homeless shelters have space for us for at least three months."

That was it. I didn't care how obnoxious an alpha it made me, my omega was *not* going to be homeless.

"I've got you, baby," I said, resting my hand on the side of Winslow's face for a split second. He only flinched a little, which was a good sign. "I've got space at my place. You two are coming home with me."

"What? No! Ty, I can't do that to you," Winslow protested. "We just met. It wouldn't be right. You have a career and a life, and Carl and I would just be a burden."

The landlord's brow shot up. "You just met? But you're...." He gestured between the two of us.

Yep, if even a random beta could sense the bond, it was a big deal.

"You're coming home with me," I told Winslow, then glanced past him to Carl—who was flipping through a book that must have been in the box by his feet. "Load everything here into the back of the truck," I called to him. "We'll find a place to store it on the mountain, then we'll come back in a few days to get the rest of your furniture and things."

"Um, the furniture belongs to the apartment," the landlord said. "That stays here."

"Whatever," I said, done with the man.

"I...guess I'll go pack our clothes," Winslow said with a sheepish roll of his shoulders. "Would that be okay, Mr. Caruthers?"

It broke my heart to see Winslow so subservient to the

man who had given away his home while he'd been stuck in the middle of heat.

"Sure, Winslow," the landlord said with a sympathetic smile. "Take all the time you need."

That bit of kindness alone kept me from strangling the life out of the man.

While Winslow went inside to pack his and Carl's clothes, I helped Carl load up the truck, which meant snapping the man out of his distractions and forcing him to stay on task.

"You owe it to your brother to get this done quickly and efficiently," I told Carl, glowering at him on purpose to try to strike the fear of God into him.

Carl dropped the box of books he'd just lifted into the bed of the truck and tried to scowl right back at me. He crumbled without me having to put any further effort into intimidating him, though.

"Look, it's not my fault," he said, letting his anxiety show. "I've tried to help him out. I've tried over and over. I swear, that website thing was a great idea, but nobody would help us out with it. Selling those supplements was a good idea too."

"I thought they were knives," I said, sliding the suitcase—which felt like it was filled with bricks—I'd taken from the porch deeper into the truck bed.

"That was a different thing," Carl said, waving like he was batting away a fly and heading back to the yard to get another load. "Everything I've tried falls flat somehow, and I've tried a lot."

"Have you tried getting a normal job at a store or a warehouse or something?" I asked, trying not to sound sarcastic.

"Yes," Carl barked at me, then bent over to snatch up a lamp that was shaped like a fish. "You ever tried to get a job when your resume shows you haven't held a job for more than a couple months?"

"Then why don't you stick to something instead of quitting all the time?" I asked, heading back for a trash bag of belongings.

"I don't quit, I get fired," Carl shouted. His tone changed entirely as he went on to mumble, "I'm not good with time. I forget to show up sometimes. I don't know why. And I get distracted easily. Especially when I'm bored with the work I'm supposed to do."

I'd known the man for less than half an hour, and already I knew that.

I sighed and picked up a few more things in addition to the trash bag, taking them to the truck. There was no point in arguing with Carl or telling him he should do better, even for Winslow's sake. I had enough training in psychology to guess there was something deeper going on with Carl. He wasn't just a lazy ass, he had...something. Maybe he was on the spectrum or had some other condition. It was hard to stay angry with a man who might not be capable of managing his own life.

But of course he wasn't. It hit me as Winslow stepped out of the apartment building with two small suitcases in his hands. Winslow managed his brother's life. He had to. Even though he was younger and an omega. That was where the toughness and strength I'd seen in my omega came from. Winslow had been raised in a single-parent household, dealt with his mother's death, and was responsible for his brother.

No wonder he'd been a virgin when I took him through that first heat wave. Hell, my omega had been willing to sell his heat to support his brother. God only knew what would have happened to him if I hadn't come along when I did.

I stepped up to Winslow and took the suitcases from him. When Winslow peeked up at me, I could tell from the redness in his eyes he'd been crying. My alpha roared, and I wanted to drop everything and take Winslow in my arms, post-heat revulsion be damned, and hold him until he was convinced everything would be all right.

I would make everything alright for Winslow if it was the last thing I ever did. He was mine, no matter how that had happened, no matter what it meant for me or my life or my career.

"It's going to be okay, baby," I said, using the pet name deliberately now. "I've got you."

Winslow broke into a watery smile and nodded. "Okay," he said in a soft voice.

God, I wanted to kiss him. I needed to. But he wasn't ready yet.

"It's just the hormones," I told him instead, using my best ESA voice. "You're still bubbling with all those heat hormones. I know you wouldn't cry about this otherwise. I know you're strong and brave, and you can handle this."

Winslow burst into a flood of tears. "Stop, Ty, that's just making it worse," he said, though he laughed as he wept, which was an even bigger sign it was just the long tail of heat.

"Are you sure we want to take this with us?" Carl asked from the other side of the yard, oblivious to the exchange Winslow and I had just had. He was looking at what appeared to be a particularly ugly macrame decoration of some sort. "It's kind of awful."

"Mom made that," Winslow said, his voice tight with emotion.

Carl's expression instantly fell to sentimental regret. "Oh. Yeah. Then of course we'll take it. But I'm not so sure about this thing." He put the macrame monstrosity back on the grass, seeming to instantly forget about it, and picked up an old-fashioned clock.

Winslow sighed, which made me turn to him. "I'm sorry about him," he said, rubbing his face to wipe away his tears—which I distinctly felt was my job. "He's a bit much."

"Don't worry about it," I said. "I can handle your brother."

I risked giving Winslow a quick peck on the cheek, then carried the suitcases to the truck. I just hoped I wasn't making my omega any promises I couldn't keep. Bringing an omega into my life without warning or planning was one thing. Figuring out his beta brother was a different story altogether.

Chapter Nine

Winslow

I'd pretty much given up on the concept of normal by the time we finished loading all of my and Carl's things into the back of Ty's truck—at least the things Mr. Caruthers had hauled out to the lawn, for which he apologized, which was also weird—and the three of us slid into the cabin. I sat in the middle, like a buffer between my brother and my...I wasn't sure what to call Ty at that point.

My post-heat prickles, as I'd decided to call the aversion to touch I'd felt all day, meant I was the last person who should have been sitting in the middle in the cabin of a Ranger, but between the way Carl chatted like we needed the sound of his voice to keep the truck moving and the glower Ty wore as he made one-syllable responses to Carl, I knew I was going to have to act as a barrier to keep the two of them from starting a war.

Possibly forever.

The thought sent a shiver through me, and I hugged myself as Ty turned off the main highway leading out of Barrington and onto what looked like a backroad that wound up into the mountains.

"You okay?" Ty asked. I heard him add "baby", even though he didn't say the word. "Are you cold? I could turn the AC down."

"Are you kidding? It's hot as a witch's tit out there," Carl said, reaching for the temperature controls on the truck's dash at the same time Ty did.

"I'm fine," I said, holding my hands out just enough to get them both to pull back, but without touching either of them. "I'm not cold or hot, I'm just a little uncomfortable from the end of heat." I lowered my voice to a whisper at the end of the sentence. Carl might not have had a problem with talking about my heat openly, but I sure did.

Particularly because it still had me feeling like a stranger in my own body. I wanted to ask Ty if that was normal, if I was supposed to be feeling like my emotions were being controlled by something on the outside, something sadistic that wanted me to cry like a baby.

"It can't be that bad," Carl said, settling against the door and glancing out the window as the terrain turned rougher and the trees grew thicker. "I'm convinced that half the things I've heard about how omegas react to heat are made up or exaggerated. You were still with it when you left the house the other morning. Are we going to be staying way out here in the woods, now that we've been kicked out of the apartment? Are there bears up here in the mountains? I heard there were bears up here. What's the best way to fight off a bear? Is it making yourself as big and noisy as possible or running away?"

I rolled my eyes and glanced apologetically as Carl's mind jumped all over the place, taking his mouth with it.

Ty scowled at the road ahead and muttered, "The best way to fight off a bear is to introduce him to a nice twink."

He didn't even crack a hint of a smile, but I chuckled all the same. Ty had been so serious and in charge of things since the moment he'd picked me up in the hotel. It was nice to see a glimmer of a sense of humor from the man. It made me wonder what other things I didn't know about him.

Volumes. There were volumes of things I didn't know about Ty, I thought with a sigh as I gazed out the window at the woods. But it was okay. I could feel he was a good man, and we would have the rest of our lives to get to know—

I sucked in a breath and hugged myself tighter, not because of that thought itself, but because of how naturally it had slipped into my mind. As if a part of me had already taken for granted the idea that Ty and I were endgame instead of two guys who had only just met.

"Are you sure you're alright?" Ty asked, peeking at me before focusing on the road again long enough to make another turn.

"Yeah," I reassured him. "I swear, this whole post-heat thing is the weirdest."

Ty managed a sympathetic smile for me as we continued up the mountain. "It is," he agreed, "but it should pass by the end of the day, tomorrow morning at the latest."

"Good," I said, breathing out heavily and wriggling against the seat, like I needed to itch my back.

What I really needed, as strange as it felt, all things considered, was a hug from Ty. Even though, at that moment, his touch would have felt like being wrapped in low-grade acid. Underneath that feeling, I really needed Ty to hold me close, even if it was just for a couple of seconds.

Because as we made another turn onto a road that was marked by a big sign for the Bangers & Mash Institute, even though I had no idea where we were or what would happen to me and Carl tomorrow—or even an hour from now—I felt safe and secure. Way safer than I would have felt if Mr. Caruthers hadn't tossed us out and I'd returned from my heat days—or maybe heat daze was a better way to think of it—to the place I'd called home for more than a year.

Ty might have been a new addition to my life, but I needed to be with him. My body and soul shouted at me that everything would be alright if I just stayed with Ty.

"Whoa! Is this the Bangers & Mash Institute?" Carl asked, sitting up straighter and nearly plastering his face to the truck's window, like he was a kid arriving at Santa's workshop.

"That's what the sign said," Ty answered with a slight growl in his voice.

Carl made no indication of hearing him before charging on with, "I've heard all about this place. It's like some wild resort in the woods where omegas go to have crazy heat sex with as many alphas as they want."

"It absolutely is not," Ty said, shooting Carl a look of genuine irritation.

Again, Carl ignored him. "I've heard that they have super exclusive parties up here with, like, the biggest alpha and omega celebrities around. And that it's like a non-stop fuck-fest all the time, and they even let betas play sometimes." I didn't like the way my brother's eyes lit up at the idea.

"None of those things are true," Ty insisted, more annoyed than ever. "This is the headquarters for the Bangers & Mash organization. It's where we have our administrative offices, our training facility, and where several key employees have their homes."

Carl pulled away from the window long enough to face Ty and ask, "But a lot of sex happens up here too, right? Omegas can choose to come up to the mountain for their heat instead of getting a house call or going to a hotel, right?"

I winced at Carl's nosy enthusiasm.

"That is true," Ty sighed. "But it's not a party or a fuck-fest." He glanced briefly at Carl with a withering look, then focused on the road again. "The point of coming to the mountain for heat is absolute discretion."

Carl snorted. "That's why they call it 'coming' to the mountain, eh?"

"Carl, stop!" I elbowed him in the side despite not wanting to touch him.

And it actually felt good.

Ty sent Carl another flat look, then took a fork in the road where a sign pointed to a parking lot on one side and "Authorized Personnel Only" on the other. We were apparently authorized.

"I'm not exactly sure what to do with the two of you," Ty said, probably to keep Carl from going off on another monologue as he glanced out the window, "but before everything else, I need to report in to my bosses, since the call didn't go as planned." He peeked at me.

I hugged myself and hunched into the seat. As if I needed the reminder that I'd screwed up not only Ty's job, but his life too. He was being nice when he said he needed to figure out what to do with me and Carl. What he probably meant was that he had to figure out what he was going to do with the load of shit that had just been unceremoniously dumped on his doorstep. The one that had suddenly made it impossible to continue in a career he was passionate about and had been doing for half my life.

"It's going to be okay," Ty murmured, as if he could read my thoughts.

Because he probably could to some degree, just like I could sort of catch the gist of what he was feeling.

Fuck. Being bonded was the awkward cherry on top of the weird-ass sundae.

The authorized personnel road went on for maybe half a

mile more before ending in a small parking lot in the middle of what looked like a quiet neighborhood of cabins tucked away in a grove of trees. The whole thing looked planned and landscaped, and there was something about the place that felt settled and right to me.

Ty pulled into an empty parking space, cut the engine, then glanced to me.

"My cabin is just up that way," he said, pointing through the windshield, "but we'll head down to the main building to see if Sal and Nick are in their office before we unload anything or get settled."

"Who lives in the other cabins?" Carl asked, already reaching for the doorhandle to get out and investigate. "How far back do the cabins go? How does the plumbing work all the way up here in the mountains? Are you connected to the main grid, or does the institute have its own generators?"

I sighed, both glad that Carl's questions ended as he got out of the truck and started up to the cabins and anxious about the sort of trouble he might get into if we didn't follow him.

"I'm really sorry about him," I said, scooting to the door Carl left open. "He means well, I swear. He's just interested in everything all the time."

"Yeah, I got that," Ty said. "What do you usually do to—oh, Lord."

Ty glanced past me to where Carl was walking up to one of the cabins so he could peek through the window.

I scrambled out the passenger door, shutting it behind me, then chased after my brother. Ty was right behind me in a second, what with his long, powerful legs.

"Carl, stop it," I called to him. "Don't go looking in people's windows."

"What?" Carl turned back, then stepped away from the

cabin with a shrug. "I just wanted to see if anyone was fucking in there."

I rolled my eyes, heating with embarrassment. Only Carl would be able to somehow think that peeping was okay.

"Those are staff cabins," Ty said with an alpha growl. "Treatment cabins are much farther up the mountain, but you will *not* go looking for them," he said, pointing at Carl.

Carl flinched, which had me smirking. It served him right. "Okay, sorry," he said, holding up his hands as the three of us started along a path that headed away from the cabins. "Can't a guy just be interested in things?"

I expected Ty to tear Carl a new one, but instead he said, "If you're curious about things, I'm sure we can find a much less irritating way for you to satisfy that curiosity."

Those words not only impressed me, they shut Carl up as well. Carl stared at Ty in disbelief for a moment before smiling, shoving his hands in his jeans pockets, and continuing on without another word.

"You've got to tell me how you did that," I whispered to Ty as we followed the path out of the patch of forest and on to a collection of fancy buildings that must have been the heart of the institute.

"Do what?" Ty asked, swaying closer to me. His hand brushed mine before he pulled away.

It must have been a sign that the post-heat prickles were going away, because I didn't mind that brief touch, even though I didn't want to hold his hand...yet.

"How did you get Carl to stop being such an annoying dweeb?" I asked.

Ty cracked a smile, barely. "If you say he's a good guy, I believe you. And if he's basically good, he just needs something to occupy him so he doesn't fly off all over the place."

I smiled, my insides filling with heat and light. Ty understood what I drove myself mental trying to explain to other people. But of course he would. I could only imagine that if he was an ESA, Ty had probably also had some sort of training in psychology too. We'd never had time to get Carl diagnosed properly, but I knew there was probably an answer to how to deal with people like him somewhere.

The sense that all was well—despite being completely fucked up—and that I was in good hands, only increased as we walked into the center of the buildings. The buildings of the Bangers & Mash Institute all had the same design. They were modern and made mostly of glass, but somehow they blended into the natural landscape around them too. Maybe it was the way the glass reflected the blue of the sky and the green of the forest.

A sense of calm and comfort radiated from the cluster of buildings as well, though I couldn't figure that out either. It was like the contentment I'd felt between heat waves, when it was just Ty holding me while we were knotted, when I didn't have to worry about a thing. I knew my alpha would take care of me.

I'd chalked that whole "my alpha" thing up to heat at the time, but I was pretty sure now it was the bond. As stupid and inconvenient as that bond was, I could see its benefits. Although I wondered what it would feel like to be bonded to an alpha who wasn't as calm and immovable as Ty.

We headed into the smallest of the buildings that made up the central complex of the institute. It was clearly an office building of some sort, though I saw desks and boards in a couple of the rooms we passed that indicated they taught classes in that building too. There were cork boards with information about training classes and the whole ESA program in the hallway, almost like the boards we'd had in school.

"Wait, you're not going to make me take classes of some sort, are you?" Carl asked. "I hate school. I was never any good at it," he added.

"Why am I not surprised?" Ty asked with a low grunt.

"I doubt you'll have to take classes," I reassured him as Ty led us down a side hall that was definitely filled with offices.

"You don't know what we'll end up doing here," Carl shot back at me. "For all we know, they'll use you for some sort of freaky training purposes, and they'll have me shoveling garbage."

I sighed. "Don't be an ass."

I would have said more, but Ty stopped at an open door and knocked on the frame. "Hey guys, got a minute?" he asked whoever was in the room.

"Ty, you're back," someone said in a bright tenor.

Ty stepped into the room, gesturing for me and Carl to follow.

The room was a big, tidy office with a double desk. Two men—an alpha and an omega, judging by their appearances—sat at the desk.

The alpha started with, "How did it go—" before stopping with his mouth open and looking at me. "Oh." He glanced between me and Ty, then let out a longer, almost painful, "Ohh."

"Yeah," Ty said. He moved back to stand by my side, resting a hand on the small of my back so gently that instead of revulsion, I only felt a slight, uncomfortable buzz. "This is Winslow Grant, and that's his brother Carl."

The alpha glanced over me and Carl, then back to Ty. "Looks like we've got a lot to talk about."

"Yeah." Ty blew out a breath and rubbed a hand over his face.

The gesture and the awkwardness I felt from him made me feel awful. Really awful.

"I'm sorry," I said, gulping like I might throw up. "I didn't mean for any of this to happen. I don't even know *how* it happened. I'm just a mistake, and now I've ruined one of your employees, and I'm just so sorry."

"Oh, honey, no, no, no." The omega leapt up from his desk and came over to take my hand. He rested his free hand on my cheek for a second and said, "When something like this happens, it's always meant to be, and it's always a good thing, I promise you."

For some reason, I didn't mind the omega touching me at all. He was old enough to be my dad, but he had a light, fun feeling about him. His hazel eyes were the kindest thing I'd ever seen. I immediately felt at ease with him.

"I'm Nicholas Mash," he said, stepping back but keeping hold of my hand, "but you can call me Nick. And this grumpy Gus is my husband, Salazar Banger, or Sal for short."

The alpha stepped forward with a look of mock irritation at being called grumpy. He glanced at his husband with absolute love, though. "My better half is right, Winslow," he said in an authoritative voice. "Bonds don't just form randomly. Especially not the sort that form instantly." He glanced to Ty with the same sort of fatherly authority and said, "There's always a reason."

Ty must have taken the statement to mean something personal. "I have that trip to Norwalk the day after tomorrow," he said, as though it were a problem.

Mr. Banger shrugged. "So? This doesn't change anything." He smiled gruffly at me.

I could tell Ty was struggling to hold things together as he said, "You know this changes everything."

"Maybe when it comes to taking ESA calls," Nick said, stepping away from me and over to his husband's side. "We'll work everything else out."

Ty wasn't satisfied with that answer. I bristled a little over the sheer fact that I knew that. I wondered if I would ever get used to knowing how someone else felt about things.

Ty glanced to me as if he was thinking the same thing—it dawned on me that feeling someone else's emotions must have been new to him too, as experienced as he was with everything else—then back to his bosses.

"I have a full client roster that will need to be shifted to someone else," he said. "This trip to Norwalk is important. Norwalk needs a B&M branch. Sanchez and Cross are expecting an alpha who can handle the initial client load, not just someone to push pencils and make phone calls."

"We'll work something out," Nick said, waving Ty's concerns away as though they were trivial.

They weren't trivial. I could feel it. I wasn't entirely sure what Ty was talking about, but I had the feeling suddenly bonding with me had done more to throw a wrench in his career plans than just making it impossible for him to be an ESA anymore. He had something else in the works, maybe a promotion of some sort, and I got the feeling I'd ruined that.

"I'm really sorry," I whispered, glancing mournfully at Ty.

Ty managed a half-hearted smile. "Don't worry about it, baby."

But I was going to worry about it, no matter what he told me to do.

"Winslow and his brother were just evicted from their apartment," Ty went on, shifting his stance and assuming the sort of take-charge alpha tone that made me feel like everything would be okay, even when I knew it wouldn't be. "Obviously Winslow would be moving in with me anyhow, but Carl needs a place to stay, too. At least until we can work something out for him."

Ty's words seemed simple, but a dozen kinds of panic washed over me. Was he going to try to get rid of Carl? I'd never lived apart from Carl before. And yeah, I'd always known we would have our own lives someday, but we'd been through so much together—Mom struggling with us on her own, her cancer, trying to live after that. The part of me that wanted to build a nest with my alpha—and maybe even consider having kids—was tiny compared to the part of me that had always had my brother by my side.

Ty turned to me, his brow going up a little, and I knew he'd felt those thoughts.

"Of course, Carl can stay with you here," Nick said, smiling at Carl.

Carl had moved to the desk and picked up a round, glass paperweight with a figure of a fox embedded inside. He was turning the thing over and over, and when he realized attention was on him, he asked, "How'd they get the fox inside the glass?"

"Very carefully," Mr. Banger said, plucking the paperweight from Carl's hand with a frown.

Nick hummed, then glanced to me, as if asking what Carl's deal was.

"Would we be able to use one of the storage lockers?" Ty asked, frowning at Carl. "I've got a load of their belongings in the back of my truck, and I won't have space for it all in my cabin."

"Sure," Mr. Banger said. "I'm sure we've got one or two empty. Let me just get you a key."

Mr. Banger headed past us to the hall. Ty followed.

"Come on," he said, mostly to Carl, who was about to pick up a book from the corner of the desk. "You're going to help me unload the truck."

"Okay," Carl said, abandoning the book and heading out the door.

I started to go too, but Nick stopped me with, "It's going to be okay, sweetie. No matter how this bond happened, Ty is a great guy, and he'll take good care of you." He smiled. "I've actually had my fingers crossed for him finding someone for years. I think this is all fantastic."

I tried to smile, but I didn't feel it at all.

"Except for the part where I've ruined his career and his life," I said, my shoulders dropping.

"Nonsense," Nick laughed. "There's far more to B&M than taking omegas through heat. Ty will realize that soon enough. We couldn't run this thing without him."

I smiled, but didn't have time to ask more. I could feel Ty walking farther away from me, and every inch of that distance made me anxious. I had to be near him, so I hurried out to the hall to catch up.

I hoped Nick was right, but I knew how important being an ESA was to Ty. He didn't want a desk job, he wanted what he'd spent ten years building. Thanks to me, he was going to have to give up his dream and settle for something else.

Chapter Ten

Ty

The first tiny glimmer of hope I had that I might be able to sort through the tangle I'd fallen into was Carl's surprising ability to focus when he was given a specific task. Unloading the truck and taking everything to one of the storage lockers contained in a building between the cabins and the heart of the complex went surprisingly well. I suspected the length of the walk between where my truck was parked and the storage building, and the fact that there wasn't much but forest between the two spots, had something to do with it.

Once everything was unloaded and Winslow was busy unpacking the suitcases, I managed to catch Carl right before he started exploring the closets in my hallway.

"You aren't going to give your brother any more of a headache than he already has, are you?" I phrased the question more like a demand.

Carl blinked at me in total surprise. "What's that supposed to mean?"

"I need your help to make this transition as smooth as possible," I said, partially ignoring his question. "It's a huge change for Winslow, and for you too."

It was a massive change for me as well, but I wasn't sure Carl had the capacity to appreciate that.

Carl turned away from the closet, as if abandoning the idea of exploring it, and crossed his arms. "Stop talking to me like I'm some sort of concrete block tied around Winslow's feet. I'm not a waste of space."

I winced inwardly, guessing that someone—maybe more than one someone—had called Carl that before.

I took a deep breath, at a loss for how to carry on and make things right for my omega.

"I'm sorry we got off on the wrong foot," I said, keeping my voice down so Winslow wouldn't hear me in the next room. "But I need you to step up and help your brother out."

"I've been trying to help him," Carl said, prickling and defensive. "I always try to help him."

"By telling him to go out onto the street to sell his heat?" I needed to let bygones be bygones, but pushing Winslow out when he was so vulnerable set every one of my alpha instincts roaring.

"We needed to pay the rent," Carl said, his expression flashing back and forth between anger and regret so fast that I could hardly keep up with it. "He could have gotten hundreds of dollars for just a couple of days. It would have helped."

"Do you have any idea what it's like for an omega in heat?" I demanded.

As soon as the question was out of my mouth, I pulled back. No. A beta like Carl wouldn't have the first clue what it was like. Carl had tunnel vision when it came to his choices. A couple hours of knowing him was enough to make that obvious. But he wasn't a bad person.

"That's all over and done with anyhow," I said, stepping back and shaking my head. "And you don't have to worry about Winslow going forward, because he's mine now. You just have to worry about taking care of yourself."

From the way Carl's eyes went wide and the bob of his Adam's apple as he swallowed, you would have thought that was the worst thing I'd said yet.

"Winslow wouldn't know what to do without me," he said, his voice hoarse.

I stared back at him. More like Carl wouldn't know what to do without Winslow.

I was going to have to figure something out for both of them. Wrapping my arms around Winslow and declaring, "Mine!" to the world wasn't going to cut it. I'd picked up an extra problem right along with Winslow, one that might just prove to be harder to figure out than how to bring an omega into my life.

"I'll tell you what," I said, trying to think rationally. "I'm going to need you to get a cot from the other storage building, the one on the upper path."

"I don't have the first clue where that is," Carl muttered. I had a feeling he was masking his anxiety with belligerence.

"I know," I said. "That's why I want you to go back to the office building, where we met Sal and Nick earlier, and ask one of them to show you where you need to go or to get someone to help you. Can you do that?"

It was a legitimate question. I wanted to see how well Carl followed directions. If he got distracted along the way or got himself into trouble, I would have a better picture of what I might have to do to settle Carl into a situation that would work for all of us.

"Yeah," Carl said, letting out a breath, his shoulders dropping. "I can do that."

"Good."

I reached out to thump his shoulder, but judging by the scowl Carl gave me, he didn't appreciate the gesture. Whatever. As long as he did what I needed him to do.

It helped that he gave me a bit of time alone with Winslow as he headed out of the cabin and along the path to the office building too. I watched through the window to make sure Carl didn't get immediately distracted, and when I was satisfied that he was on task, I headed back to the bedroom, where I'd quickly cleared out a drawer in my bureau for Winslow's clothes.

As soon as I stepped into the room, my heart lurched in my chest. Winslow was asleep on my bed, curled over on his side, still fully dressed with his sneakers on. He was the picture of exhausted innocence as he breathed slowly and steadily, his lips parted just a bit.

I fought to ignore the rush of lust that hit me as I remembered what those lips felt like wrapped around my cock. I let myself drink in the sight of his round ass filling out his jeans beautifully. My heart gave another lurch at the faint spot of dampness on the seat of his jeans. That was me. He still had my seed inside him. I should have stopped somewhere to pick him up some post-heat pads, but we'd had too many other things on our minds.

And besides, that tiny indication that I'd had him, that he was still filled with me, gave me a deep sense of satisfaction, whether it was right or not.

I headed to the bed, pausing to take off my shoes halfway, then moved to sit by Winslow's side. As carefully as I could, not wanting to wake him, I pulled at his shoelaces, then eased his sneakers off. Winslow snuffled in his sleep, then rolled to his other side so he was facing me. He still clutched his arms to his chest, which made his change of position both endearing and defensive.

I inched farther up the bed so I could brush his hair back from his forehead. That slight touch was enough to make me smile instinctively. Winslow was so beautiful, though I had a feeling he didn't know it. His face was perfectly formed, his nose turned up just enough to give him character, and his lips were lush and inviting. It wasn't just the bond or my alpha instincts telling me so either. Winslow had a sweet, attractive look that could charm anyone.

I was lucky I'd found him when I did. In more ways than one. Looking the way he did, radiating heat as ferociously as he had been, he could have been snatched up and put through unspeakable horrors.

But I was also lucky to have found someone I connected with instantly. I still didn't understand why or how it had happened. Maybe Winslow's confession that I'd been his first had something to do with it. Bonds usually only formed when two people were deeply compatible. I was looking forward to figuring out what it was that made us so compatible.

It was a risk to climb over Winslow and to lie down so that I could pull him into my arms. He was still at that point post-heat where my touch might cause him discomfort. But instead of scrambling away, he flipped over to face me again and all but burrowed into me, nuzzling his face against my neck, like he had when I'd first picked him up. Logically, I knew that gesture was because my scent was strongest where my skin was exposed. Emotionally, it felt like acceptance.

We stayed like that for maybe ten minutes before Winslow woke with a start and wriggled away from me.

"Sorry," I said, immediately sitting up and holding up my hands so he knew I meant him no harm. "I know you're probably not ready yet. I literally couldn't resist."

Winslow rubbed his face groggily, then glanced up at me

with those beautiful, lost eyes of his. "No, it's fine. I...I'm feeling better about the whole touching thing. I just...didn't know where I was for a second."

"You're home," I said, then immediately wanted to roll my eyes at myself for being a sentimental fool.

But Winslow smiled shyly in answer. "I'm still trying to wrap my head around that."

"Take all the time you need," I said, climbing off the far side of the bed. To ease the awkwardness of the moment, I pretended to be casual as I said, "Do you want lunch? I'm sure I have stuff to make sandwiches in my fridge."

"Yeah," Winslow said, slipping off the other side of the bed.

His face pinched as his feet hit the floor, and I could tell from his body language—and the bond—that he could feel what was going on with his ass.

"Um," he mumbled, looking sheepishly at me, "would you mind if I took another shower?"

"Go right ahead," I said, nodding to the en suite bathroom. "Take your time. It's completely normal," I added. "I can run over to my friend Chris's cabin across the way while you're in there to get some post-heat pads. Chris is an omega."

I could see a hundred questions in Winslow's eyes before he nodded silently. My guess was that he wondered whether I'd slept with Chris, in heat or out of it. It was a typical bonded omega, jealous reaction, and I thought it was kind of sweet.

But since I actually had taken Chris through heat a couple years ago, I wasn't going to say a damn thing.

Winslow turned to the bathroom, then turned back to ask, "Where's Carl?"

"I send him on an errand," I said. "I'm interested to see if he'll follow instructions."

Winslow looked as though I'd pulled the pin out of a grenade. "This should be interesting."

"That's the impression I have too," I said with a lopsided grin.

Winslow went on to take his shower, and I headed out to get what I needed from Chris. I saw no sign of Carl as I glanced down the path to the center of the complex, but that didn't mean anything. I wasn't sure what the state of the spare cots was, which meant the whole thing could easily take longer than a couple minutes.

I was lucky that Chris was home, that he had pads, and that he didn't ask too many questions as he handed them over. I took them home to Winslow, then set to work tidying things up and moving furniture to make room for the cot in my office. It was supposed to be a second bedroom anyhow, so if Carl ended up living with us for longer than—

Nope. I didn't want to think about that. I had to find another situation for Carl. This thing with Winslow was new, and I wanted time to get to know my omega.

We would probably have to find a bigger place anyhow, my thoughts went on as I put together some sandwiches. My cabin was fine for a bachelor, but when Winslow and I had kids—

Nope. I wasn't going to think about that either. I still had to figure out what the fuck I was going to do about the career I'd just shredded. Depending on how things went, I might need to hatch the sort of schemes Carl seemed prone to just to keep a roof over my and Winslow's head.

But the time Winslow came out of the bedroom, washed and dressed in clean clothes, looking and smelling like a dream, I'd talked myself back into good sense. Sal and Nick wouldn't fire me. They'd find a way to keep me on at B&M. I wasn't going to be homeless or jobless. I just wouldn't be doing the thing I thought I'd been born to do, or that was my lifelong passion.

"This looks good. What is it?" Winslow asked as he sat at the kitchen table and picked up a sandwich.

"You've never had ham salad?" I asked.

Winslow shook his head and took a bite. Immediately, his face lit up...and my heart pinged like someone had plucked a guitar string.

"It's good," he said with his mouth half full, then took another bite. "I like it."

"I'm glad," I said, sounding calm and even banal on the outside. Inside, I was puffed up with pride over having provided for my omega and making him smile.

Lunch actually turned out to be good. The sense of satisfaction I felt over feeding and taking care of Winslow was more than I was ready for. It was the same sense of a job well done that I'd felt at the end of my ESA calls for the past ten years...times a million.

The only fly in the ointment was Carl. He didn't come back in time for lunch. He didn't come back during the entire post-lunch nap Winslow took on the couch in my living room while I caught up on some of the paperwork I always had to fill out after a call, or when I called Mr. Caruthers to make arrangements to pick up the rest of Winslow's and Carl's things after the trip to Norwalk.

I was really starting to worry and contemplate going off in search of Carl when he finally burst through the front door, dragging one of the big cots with him.

"You'll never guess where I've been," Carl said, focusing in on Winslow—who had just awakened from his nap.

"Where have you been?" Winslow asked, but not in a tone that fit Carl's statement. "It's...it's after four o'clock," he said, looking at the clock over my fireplace.

"I see you found a cot," I said, getting up from the sofa.

Winslow had been sleeping with his legs over mine—which seemed to surprise him a little—and I had to swing his legs to the side to stand.

"Yeah, I did," Carl told me with a challenging look. "And before you start accusing me of being useless and getting off-task, I went straight to the office building, like you told me to, and Nick needed my help putting together some booklets for the next ESA training class. So no, I didn't wander off into the woods or get eaten by a bear or anything, okay?"

Again, I had the feeling that burst of verbal diarrhea came from Carl being accused of all those things before.

"Okay, okay," I said, crossing to take the cot from him. "Let me show you where to set this up."

Carl gave up the cot reluctantly and followed me into the office. I unfolded it and started the process of setting it up, then showed him the linen closet and told him to finish with the set-up himself while I got dinner started. Carl started out well enough, but when I went to check on him after fifteen minutes, he'd gotten distracted by a tavern puzzle I'd been given at the B&M Christmas party's Secret Santa gift exchange. I figured that was a harmless diversion, so I left him to it and continued with supper.

Winslow kept me company in the kitchen through the prep, even chopping vegetables and setting the table for me. He was quiet, though. A little too quiet. I'd ascribed his slight withdrawal after his nap as leftover grogginess and heat exhaustion, but when he didn't seem to bounce back, even during supper, when Carl chattered on about helping Nick and fetching the cot from the storage building, I knew something was wrong.

There were several possibilities of things that were keeping Winslow quiet and hunched in on himself through supper. I immediately dismissed the idea that he'd somehow gotten pregnant during heat, despite the precautions we'd taken. His heat would have ended more abruptly if he had, and he wouldn't have experienced the aversion to touch. Quite the opposite. If I'd knocked him up, he would be clingy and purring.

It was also possible that he was still exhausted and embarrassed over everything. Winslow struck me as a sensitive soul, even without heat, and as the kind of people pleaser that didn't want to make trouble for anyone. I could feel all those emotions through our bond as we finished up supper and cleared the table. I sent Carl to go watch TV while Winslow and I put the leftovers away and loaded the dishwasher, hoping that would give Winslow an opening to share his feelings, but he still kept whatever it was to himself.

It wasn't until the cop show Carl had picked for us all to watch was over and I stood up from the couch, holding out my hand to Winslow, that I had a hint of what was going on.

"Come on, baby. You look so tired. It's time to go to bed," I said.

Winslow blinked up at me in surprise. "I...I thought I was going to sleep on the couch."

Carl opened his mouth like he was going to comment, but one frown from me and he snapped his mouth shut again.

"No, sweetheart, I want you sleeping with me," I said. Part of me winced at how alpha that sounded, but dammit, that's what I was. Even more so now.

"You do?" Winslow mumbled, his face flushing pink.

"Of course," I said, trying to sound tender and considerate instead of bossy and possessive. A thought struck me, and I said, "If you would prefer to sleep on the couch, that's fine."

I watched Winslow consider it for a few seconds before pushing himself to stand. "No, I'd rather sleep in your bed."

I smiled and offered my hand. He took it, then let me lead him into the bedroom.

"I'm just going to watch some more TV," Carl called after

us. "I can turn the volume up higher if you two want to...you know."

"Keep the volume down," I told him over my shoulder with a frown. "We all need to sleep. *All* of us." I trusted he would take that as the command I intended it to be.

I'd hoped Winslow would open up once we were alone in the bedroom with the door shut, but he was still overly quiet as we got ready for bed. I let him use the bathroom first, and when he shuffled out in an old t-shirt and pajama bottoms, I took my turn. I would let the pajamas slide for the time being, I would even keep my boxers on for the night, but my omega would have to get used to sleeping nude in a hurry, because that's how I wanted—

I sighed at myself and shook my head as I used the toilet, then brushed my teeth. Those sorts of alpha thoughts were becoming more pronounced, and I was taking them for granted now. It was great, as far as building that sort of a relationship went, but it scared the fuck out of me how quickly my brain was adjusting to a life I hadn't asked for and didn't know what to do with.

I finished up in the bathroom, then found Winslow already in bed, lying on his side, with the covers pulled up to his chin. I didn't like the worried, guilty emotions I felt coming from him. I figured over twelve hours was enough for him to be over the worst of the touch aversion, so when I climbed in bed with him, I pulled him into my arms.

Winslow surprised me by snuggling up against me and throwing an arm over my chest. I forced myself to breathe steadily and not to demand that he tell me everything he was thinking, or to order him to be relaxed and comfortable with me. He would tell me what was wrong in his own time.

But waiting for him to trust me enough to be honest with his feelings just might drive me up a wall.

Chapter Eleven

Winslow

The first thing I felt as I woke up to early-morning light peeking around the edges of the curtains was a sense of deep contentment and safety. It really wasn't like anything I'd ever felt before. Of course, everything in the last four days was like nothing I'd ever felt before, but that sensation of absolute calm and rightness was profound. The only thing I could think of that came anywhere close was what I must have felt as a very small child, with Mom cuddling and cooing over me.

It wasn't really a good comparison, since, right along with the peace at my core were feelings that were definitely sexual, but the way that sense of rightness seemed to pulse through me with every beat of my heart and fill me with every breath I took was heady. It wasn't just me, either. My insides, my heart and soul, were entwined with Ty. I could feel our impossible bond, really feel it.

And then I woke up the rest of the way.

That's when the guilt and panic of the situation took over from all the good, soft feelings.

I was in a virtual stranger's bed. I had blasted into his life like a wrecking ball and destroyed his career, his lifelong dream. I didn't even know what I wanted to do with my life and my future, and I'd upended Ty's life so that he probably didn't have a clue what he would do next either. Without even trying, I'd ruined everything.

I forced myself not to clench up and to continue to breathe deeply. Something told me that if I let my reactions get too big, Ty would feel them. Then he would wake up—and I'd ruin his sleep along with everything else—and demand to know what was wrong. *Then* I'd be forced to admit to him that he'd ended up bonded to a lump of nothing who didn't even know what he wanted to be when he grew up.

I shifted a little, intending to roll away from Ty to give him some space. It was unbelievable that I'd somehow snuggled up against him and lay half draped over him to begin with. The handful of times I'd slept in the same bed with someone before, I'd never wanted them touching me in my sleep. Now, I had a hard time with the idea of detaching from Ty. So much so that I couldn't do it, even though I knew I should.

Which meant I was left there plastered against him, my cheek against his shoulder, a bit of his chest hair tickling my chin, my hand resting over his steadily beating heart, one of my knees hiked up over his thigh.

I closed my eyes again and let out a breath. What was I going to do now? Hardly anyone my age was bonded to an alpha. No one I'd gone to school with was even married, and only one or two were in committed relationships. This whole thing had come out of the blue, and I had no idea what to do with it. I hadn't honestly imagined myself with someone else. Like, ever. I didn't have anything to offer. Yeah, I'd gotten good grades in high school, but I hadn't been able to afford college, and even if I had, I didn't have the first clue what I wanted to study.

I took another breath and tried to pull it together. I was here now, with Ty and at the Bangers & Mash facility. From the sound—and the feel—of things, Ty wasn't going to give me up. I was a good worker. I hadn't lost my last couple of jobs because I sucked at them or because I couldn't do the work. There had to be something at the Bangers & Mash facility that I could do. I could help out in the office, filing stuff or making copies or whatever. Or, hell, I could be a custodian and take out the trash, or clean up the cabins that were used for heats.

I started to breath a little easier. It wasn't a complete loss. Just because I didn't have the sort of drive or sense of purpose Ty had, that spark of whatever it was that inspired people to follow their passion and have a career, didn't mean I was completely useless. I could work hard, do whatever Ty told me to do.

I swallowed hard, a shiver passing through me. I would do *whatever* Ty told me to do. Even stuff in bed. Even though that kind of terrified me a little. Heat was one thing, but Ty was the only guy I'd ever been with, the only sex I'd ever had. What would it mean to put myself completely at the mercy of a massive, powerful alpha who could use me like a rag whenever he got an itch? I'd done a lot of things in heat that made me blush to think about now. Could I do all those things and keep my alpha happy that way when I wasn't in heat?

It was too unnerving to think about. Enough so that I was finally able to inch away from Ty and roll out of bed silently. I tucked the covers around Ty before tip-toeing out of the room and down the hall to the bathroom. I didn't want to use the en suite, because I didn't want Ty to wake up when I flushed.

I calmed down a little once I wandered into the cabin's kitchen—although the awareness of Ty stayed with me, like he was standing right behind my shoulder, and if I turned around, he'd be there, smiling at me. I tried to ignore it as I searched through the cabinets for something I could make for breakfast.

I found everything I needed to make French toast, which was usually a weekend and holiday treat for me and Carl, when we could manage it. I'd made French toast for Mom a few times when she was sick, before the chemo tore up her stomach. I could make a big, hearty breakfast for Ty now, as a way to show my appreciation, and to demonstrate that I wasn't completely useless.

Weirdly enough, the cooking calmed me down. Was that some sort of cliché omega thing that was really getting to me now that I was bonded to an alpha? Did that sort of old-fashioned TV show vibe automatically hit omegas once they'd gone through heat and been claimed by an alpha?

I winced as I flipped a batch of toast in the frying pan. God, I hoped not. I didn't want to be a cliché. I wasn't particularly domestic. Yes, I'd had to take care of Carl for the last few years, but I absolutely was not one of those omegas who popped out half a dozen kids and spent all his time at the playground, discussing chest-feeding or which brand of diaper bag was the best or which soccer coach was the hottest. More power to the omegas who liked that sort of thing, but that wasn't what I wanted to do with my life.

Not that I knew what I actually did want for my pathetic life.

"Mmm! That smell reminds me of Mom," Carl said, wandering into the kitchen, his hair a mess and his face still pink from sleep.

Carl's words sent an unexpected pang through me. I swallowed hard, slipped the pieces of toast that were finished onto a plate, and set the plate at one of the places on the table, where I'd already put the butter and syrup I'd found.

"What do you think Mom would say if she could see us now?" I asked, going back to the counter for the carafe from the coffee maker, which had just finished brewing, and taking that to the table as well.

Carl blinked, then picked up the carafe the second I put it down. "She'd be really proud of you, that's for sure," he said.

I made a sound of disagreement, then went back to the stove to start another batch of toast. "I doubt it. She'd be shocked about this whole thing with Ty."

"No, she wouldn't," Carl said, almost laughing. "She'd like Ty, and she'd think it was nice that her baby boy had someone big and strong to take care of him."

The word "baby" sent a shiver through me, reminding me of how I felt when Ty called me that. "She'd be disappointed that I ruined someone's career just by—"

I didn't finish the sentence—partially because I didn't know what, exactly, I'd done, other than waving my heat-wet ass at Ty like a strumpet, and partially because I felt Ty getting closer.

Sure enough, when I glanced over my shoulder, Ty had stepped into the kitchen.

He looked amazingly put-together for so early in the morning. He'd obviously showered already, and he was dressed in business casual. The blue of his button-down shirt complemented his skin and hair colors beautifully, and his slacks didn't quite hide the shape of his thighs or his ass.

And now I was noticing the way people dressed. No, not people, Ty. I couldn't have cared less about clothes, but I noticed every detail about him.

Bonds were weird.

"Smells good," Ty said, a smile lighting his face as he wandered over to the stove, where I was flipping the current batch of toast. "Smells very good."

He walked right up behind me, as though it were nothing,

and slipped his arms around me. He then bent down to breathe in by my neck, pulling me so that my back was flush against his chest. My ass fit a little too perfectly against the top of his thighs and the bulge in his trousers.

And I loved it.

God, I loved it so much!

A moment later, Ty caught his breath and stepped quickly away.

"I'm sorry," he said. "I don't know what came over me. I shouldn't have just assumed...."

I was pretty sure we both knew what had come over him, and I was equally sure that we were both freaked out by how natural it had felt.

"No problem," I mumbled, then nodded to the table. "I made coffee. And this is the French toast I used to make for our mom."

Somehow, bringing up Mom and drawing Carl into the discussion felt like a really effective shield against the overwhelming awkwardness that battled with my instinct to surrender to a traditional omega role.

"It looks great," Ty said, sitting stiffly at the table and reaching for the coffee. "Thank you for making breakfast."

"Winslow is great with breakfast," Carl said, eyeing Ty with a combination of suspicion and amusement that threatened to give me a headache if I watched the two of them interact for too long. "He's always been good at taking care of people. Mom and me," Carl went on. "I've been trying to tell him for years that he should go into some sort of nursing or caretaking industry. I bet if he was a home healthcare worker, he could make a ton of money."

I sighed and focused on cooking, keeping my back to the table so I wouldn't have to see either Ty's or Carl's expression. I did add, "Home healthcare workers don't actually make a lot of money," before vowing I wasn't going to get involved in the conversation.

"I guess it would really depend on their level of professional training," Ty said. A beat passed, and he added, "If that's something you wanted to explore, I would support that."

I winced, glad Ty couldn't see my face. It sounded to me like a not-so-subtle hint that I should get a job so that I wasn't a burden to him.

Although I knew it was already too late for that.

"No," I said. "I don't think that's what I want to do," I said, mumbling so that I worried he might not even hear me.

"Well, you don't have to do anything now," Carl said, diving into his French toast. "You've got yourself a sugar-alpha now, and this sweet cabin comes with the deal. You don't really have to do anything anymore."

A pinch of horror nearly made me drop the spatula. "I don't want to take advantage," I said, turning enough to meet Ty's eyes. He'd been watching me, which didn't bode well. "I'll work. I'll do whatever you need me to do. I won't be a burden to you."

Again, images of me servicing him the way I had when I was in heat flooded back to me. Did it count as being a prostitute if you did all those things for an alpha you were bonded with in exchange for room and board?

"You could never be a burden, Winslow. We don't have to figure anything out right now," Ty said in that voice I was starting to recognize as his professional calm. Like he was talking to a skittish horse. "We have all the time in the world to figure things out."

I wondered if we did, though. Ty and his bosses had said something about a business trip when we were in the office the day before. And Ty probably had an entire schedule of work that I'd just blown out of the water.

"I have a meeting in half an hour," Ty went on. "I slept late this morning, so I'm running just a little behind. But you guys are welcome to hang out here in the cabin or to take a walk in the mountains while I'm at work."

"Awesome," Carl said brightly. "I want to see if I can find the cabins where heat clients—"

"No," Ty told him so authoritatively that I felt it in my bones. "That's the one thing you're not to do. Clients come here for discretion and confidentiality. You will not wander around looking for them."

"Okay," Carl said, sounding cowed. He recovered quickly to say, "Maybe I'll go looking for bears instead."

That wasn't much better, but I knew from experience, there was no arguing with Carl when he was in a hatching ideas mood.

I finished with the French toast for Ty, presenting him with a plate, then made one last batch for myself. By the time I sat at the table to eat and have some coffee, I was feeling marginally more relaxed. Carl had taken over the conversation, of course, bouncing from the little he knew about bears to a trip to the zoo he'd made with his class in fifth grade to insisting he would have studied zoology, if he'd been able to afford college.

I was happy to let him talk, and evidently, Ty was too. Probably because Carl's incessant talking covered up the other conversation that was going on between the two of us—the one where Ty asked me with subtle looks if I was okay and if I wanted to talk about everything, and where I ignored him and pretended nothing was wrong.

"Well, I've got to get going," Ty said after we'd all finished eating, getting up to take his plate and mine to the sink. "I'll check in on you as soon as the meeting is over, before they get me to do anything else. And if you need anything, I'll be in the administration building, right near Sal and Nick's office. Don't hesitate to come and get me."

"Okay," I said, then instinctively tilted my cheek up as Ty walked past and bent down to kiss it.

We both froze, the same way we had at the stove earlier. At least he felt jerked around by instinct and our bond too. It was so bizarre to do things like we'd already established a routine when we hadn't even known each other for a week.

"Come get me if you need me," Ty repeated in a slightly strained voice, then hurried out of the room.

I didn't move, I barely breathed, until I heard the cabin door shut. Then I let out a heavy breath.

"Is that the whole bond thing at work?" Carl asked. "Because you're not usually all cutesy and housematey like that."

"Yeah, tell me about it," I said, getting up and starting to clear the rest of the table.

"If that's the sort of thing that happens to omegas when they go through heat, then I'm glad you didn't find someone to pay you for yours," Carl said, helping himself to another cup of coffee instead of getting up to tidy the kitchen with me. "Who knows what kind of loser we would have ended up with if that had happened?"

I twisted from where I'd just put some dishes in the sink to glare at him. I almost opened my mouth to shout that "we" did not end up with anyone, "I" was the one who had accidentally bonded with an alpha I barely knew, and that I had no idea what my life looked like or was supposed to be now.

The problem was, Carl looked completely unbothered by the situation. More than that, he looked relaxed for the first time in a long time.

As well he should be. Already, Ty had demonstrated that he might be willing to take responsibility for Carl and not just me. I could feel as weird and uncomfortable as I wanted, but

Ty might just be able to do the one thing that I'd never been able to do. He might be able to keep Carl out of trouble somehow.

But what did I have to give him in return?

"I don't know what's going to happen," I said, letting out a breath and busying myself with cleaning up. "I just hope Mr. Banger and Mr. Mash don't fire Ty because he can't be an ESA anymore."

"They won't," Carl said with way more surety than I felt. "Mr. Mash said so yesterday."

"Yeah, but that doesn't mean—" I gave up, figuring it was pointless to worry about what would or wouldn't happen once Ty's bosses realized the full impact of what I'd done.

I cleaned up the kitchen, and when that was done, I moved on to the main room. The cabin was a good size with big rooms, but there weren't a lot of them. There was the kitchen, the two bedrooms, the hall bathroom and the en suite, and a big, open living room with a fireplace. As Carl wandered off to shower, I did my best to straighten the main room.

Was that what I was now? Was I just a housemate, like Carl had said? I kind of hated the idea. I'd thought I had more ambition than that. But honestly, the last five years of my life had been taking care of Mom, then Carl, and just holding it together with whatever stupid job would hire me.

Could I even have a job or a career, like Ty used to have until I'd come along? Or would Ty demand that we not use protection next time I went into heat so that he could knock me up? It was a cliché that omegas all wanted to have babies, but that didn't mean it was also a cliché that all alphas wanted to spread their seed and keep their omegas pregnant all the time.

Just thinking about it gave me a headache. And as I forced myself to straighten the main room, that headache grew. This wasn't the life I'd envisioned for myself. It wasn't what I wanted.

"You know, we could really make the best of this," Carl said as he came out of the second bedroom, clean and dressed and speaking as if we'd been having a conversation since getting up from the breakfast table. "Being attached to an alpha like this could really open doors for us."

I grimaced, pressing my fingertips to my temples to try to ease the pain of my now pounding head. Somehow, Carl's mention of Ty, even vaguely, made my body hurt.

"Ty isn't your cash cow, Carl," I said, moving to the couch to sit down. "You're not here to take advantage of him."

"No, but seriously," Carl rushed to sit on the couch with me. "This could be a great opportunity. Next time I go looking for investors for that website idea, I could say that I have the backing of an alpha. Those things still carry a lot of weight with some people."

"You're not investing in any websites," I said, starting to feel like I couldn't breathe. "You're not going to cause any more trouble for Ty than I've already caused. You're going to find a job of some sort and learn to support yourself on your own."

"Yeah, of course," Carl said, waving his hand as if brushing away what I'd said—which surprised me, really. I'd thought he would object more to me telling him to support himself. "I'm just saying that having an alpha in the family opens a lot of doors."

I stood abruptly, not completely sure why. "I need to go find him," I blurted before I thought about it. "Something's wrong and I need to be near him."

"It's probably the bond thing," Carl said, jumping up with me. "You shouldn't be alone right now."

I had the feeling Carl was right, but as I rushed to the cabin door and burst out into the crisp, mountain morning, I sent him a frown over my shoulder. I loved my brother, really, I did, but why couldn't he take responsibility for his own life and leave me and my alpha to live our own?

I growled to myself as the automatic thought hit me. I had a life with someone other than Carl or my mom now. Forces within me compelled me to that life in a major way. I just wish I knew what that life entailed and how I was supposed to live it.

Chapter Twelve

Ty

I knew what the problem was even before I left the cabin and started down the path to the office. The pain started behind my eyes and deep in my chest, deeper than my heart. I shouldn't have left Winslow alone when he was feeling uncertain about himself and the situation we'd landed in. Bonded pairs always felt just a little uncomfortable when they were apart from each other—like they'd accidentally put on the other one's underwear, and it just didn't fit right—but that sensation was always much, much worse when the bond was new, and when one or both of the partners in a bonded pair was upset about something. I'd been working for B&M long enough and had enough friends who had bonded to know all about it.

By the time I reached the administration building and threw open the door with way more force than I needed to, it was like someone was stabbing daggers into the back of my eyes. Winslow was anxious about everything that had happened between us, and about where we would go from here. I'd known that from before we went to bed last night, but, like the idiot I was, I'd left him at the cabin to go to work. I hadn't thought anything of it, because I'd always just walked away from the end of my ESA calls without feeling any sort of lingering attachment to the omega. I should have known from the start what was happening.

"Morning, Ty," Nick greeted me as I walked into the conference room we were using for our meeting and straight to the coffee maker that had been set up in one corner. "How did things go with—oh."

I didn't need to look at Nick to see that he could tell I was experiencing bond pain. Nick and Sal had been married for almost thirty years and bonded for most of that time, so they, of all people, would know bond pain when they saw it.

Sure enough, when I turned around after pouring a black coffee, Nick looked at me with deep sympathy, and Sal had a typically alpha frown that passed for understanding of an uncomfortable emotion he knew a little too well.

"It's fine," I said, walking to the conference table and sitting at one of the chairs facing the window. I couldn't see my cabin from this side of the building, but even looking out at the trees eased some of the frustration that pounded in my head. "I'll be fine. I'm trying not to let this affect things."

That was a loaded statement if ever there were one. I could try all I wanted, but everyone in that room knew that everything had changed.

"It gets easier with time," Phillip—my longtime friend and coworker, and Nick and Sal's son—said as he took a seat at the table across from me. "When Jesse and I first bonded, I had to leave the mountain to go stay at his place overnight until the connection mellowed out a little. Thank God it did, or else I'd be auditing high school math classes right about now." He laughed.

I tried to smile. Jesse taught math in Barrington at Olivarez High School, and since they'd bonded, they'd officially tied the knot and bought a house midway between town and the mountain to be halfway between both of their jobs.

Actually, Phillip and Jesse where exactly the people I needed to talk to. They'd bonded accidentally during a heat that had snuck up on Phillip and trapped the two of them together in unusual circumstances last year. They might have some insights into unexpected bonding that would help me and Winslow.

"What's this I hear about you bonding with a client?" Garrett, another alpha who worked in administration, along with being an ESA, asked as he strode into the room. "It's all over the mountain."

I sighed and rubbed my forehead. That was exactly what I didn't want to happen. And as more members of our planning team entered the room for the meeting, I knew it was only going to get worse.

"It's true," I told Garrett, aware the others were looking on. "I bonded with an omega, but he wasn't a client. He was in distress at the Grand Hotel, so I took him up to the room and helped him through his heat. It was his first heat."

I don't know why I added that last bit, but my coworkers hummed and nodded, as though they understood everything now. Even Gloria, who was a beta.

She was a psychologist, though, which was probably what gave her the authority to say, "That sense of coming to his rescue could have opened you for some sort of bond."

"But they would have to have some kind of basic, fundamental compatibility in order for a bond to form," Ainsley, an omega who had been with B&M almost as long as I'd been pointed out. She shifted to face Nick and asked, "Bonds don't just randomly form between two people with nothing at all in common, right?"

"Right," Nick said, taking one of the two seats at the head of the table. Sal sat in the other one, and Nick touched him almost absentmindedly before continuing with, "No one really understands the science behind it, but people only bond if they are really and truly a good match."

"I've never heard of a single case of people who don't actually get along bonding," Sal said with a shrug, as though it could still happen, but hadn't happened yet.

"Sounds to me like you were extraordinarily lucky to find this omega," Gloria said with a smile. "What's his name again?"

"Winslow," I answered, feeling a swell of fondness...that immediately had me out of sorts, since it was such an unusual emotion for me. "But I'd rather get started discussing this trip to Norwalk than talking about my personal life," I said, then plowed straight on to, "If you all decide you want someone else to handle the negotiations with Cross and Sanchez, I completely understand."

A chorus of protest rose up from the room as the others all took their places. I hated that kind of attention, and I especially hated the sympathy that went along with it. Alpha pride might have been a cliché, but I really felt it in that moment.

"You've been working on this project for months now," Garrett said taking the seat next to me. "Why would anyone want to pull you off the job now?"

I stared at him with harsh frankness. "I can't give my clients what they need anymore," I said, meaning that on more than one level.

A soft hush settled over the table as the others took their seats and organized their notes and notebooks.

Garrett seemed to catch onto the elephant in the room as far as my position with B&M was concerned. He sucked in a breath, then nodded slowly. A moment after that, he said, "Just because you can't take clients anymore doesn't mean you're not the absolute best person to set up the deal for this branch in Norwalk."

"It might," I said, writhing in my chair—not only because of the focus on me personally, but because I could feel Winslow, feel him out there, needing me. My head throbbed, and my body felt bruised. "Norwalk can only put so much money into this project," I told the others. Pretending this was just another business meeting with problems to be solved was the only thing I could do to take my mind off the pain. "Sanchez and Cross are putting up the rest of the money out of their own personal finances. That means they needed me not only to iron out the deal and to head up the new office, they needed me to continue as a hands-on ESA as well. They can't afford to pay additional staff. Everyone who ends up transferring out there—if the deal goes through—is going to need to do double duty until the branch starts to make a profit."

The moments of silence that followed my explanation told me that the others were starting to see the dilemma.

"It wouldn't be right to take you off this project," Sal said at last, breaking the silence and easing some of my tension at the same time. "You know more about what's going on with this deal than anyone. Besides which, there isn't time to have someone else take over as point person, since you're expected in Norwalk tomorrow."

"But are Sanchez and Cross even going to want to listen to me if I start out the meeting by changing the terms of the deal that we've already talked about?" I asked.

"We won't know that until you're there, or until you've talked this through with them," Nick said. "I spoke to Madeline Cross yesterday afternoon, and she has a few reservations about the changes, but she and her husband still want to meet with you."

That came as a surprise to me—both that Nick had already spoken to them and that they still wanted to meet. It was a step in the right direction and maybe a positive sign for B&M overall, but I still didn't see how I could possibly fit into the picture of the new branch if I couldn't continue on as an ESA.

I couldn't see how I would fit at B&M the way I'd always assumed I would if I couldn't continue as an ESA. Helping omegas was my passion. Helping one in particular had yanked the rug out from under me.

"I just want to put it out there that I am willing to hand this whole thing over to someone else, if that's what you all think is best," I said, glancing around the room at my coworkers. I hesitated, then pushed on with, "And if you think it's best that I step down from B&M entirely, since my usefulness to the company has drastically changed, then I accept that decision too."

My offer to quit was immediately met with protest.

"You can't quit," Ainsley said. "You're essential to this company."

"Just because you can't take calls anymore doesn't mean there isn't a place here for you," Phillip agreed.

"You can't just throw away ten years of experience like that," Garrett argued.

My stomach turned at his comment, and I put down my cup of coffee before taking a sip. Ten years of experience out the window. It hurt.

No, what hurt was being apart from Winslow. That was where my clouded thinking was coming from. Everything that had happened in the last few days was too new and too unexpected for me to be thinking clearly about my place in the company and the rest of my life. And chances were, I was still dealing with the effects of heat hormones. It was just incredibly hard to bend to the whims of fate when I'd spent my entire life making solid decisions and deciding my own course in life.

"I don't think we should make any changes to the trip or our offer to Sanchez and Cross just yet," Sal said, taking charge of the meeting. "For now, we proceed exactly the way we'd planned. It wouldn't be fair to the client, or to the city of Norwalk, to make any sort of decision about how their branch should be run, or if they want to continue with the project, without talking to them first. Now, Garrett, let's hear those financials you've been working on."

Sal was right, and it was a relief to think that I didn't have to make all the decisions on the whole thing quite yet. Still, I couldn't help but feel like everything I'd built was slipping through my fingers.

The sense that I needed to take charge, that I couldn't let everything important get away from me, increased with every breath I took, and so did the pounding in my head. Not only couldn't I focus on what Garrett was saying as the meeting continued, I began to have a hard time keeping my irrational panic that something was horribly wrong at bay.

Only a handful of minutes later, I knew that Winslow was near. The sensation was strong enough that by the time he skidded to a stop in the open doorway of the conference room, panting as if he'd run from the cabin, I was already halfway out of my chair.

I nearly knocked the chair over in my haste to reach the doorway and throw my arms around Winslow. "It's okay, baby. I've got you now," I said without thinking.

It was like taking the lid off a pot and releasing all the steam and pressure. All of the muscles in my body that I'd subconsciously clenched relaxed as I pressed Winslow against me, cradling the side of his head and breathing in his lollipop scent. Winslow let out a groan of relief as well, which only made me hug him tighter.

Until I realized that the entire conference room of my peers was watching us with varying degrees of sentiment or embarrassment. I hated both emotions—the idea that they thought Winslow and I were cute and the way we'd embarrassed some of them with our affection. Especially since everything I felt—and probably that Winslow felt too—still had that awkwardness of being imposed on us by some force on the outside.

I cleared my throat and stood straighter, gently nudging Winslow out of my arms. I slipped his hand into mine, though. I couldn't detach from him entirely. "Everyone, I'd like you to meet Winslow Grant," I said. And then, because he'd stumbled up to the room and was now hovering behind us, peeking over my and Winslow's shoulders to see what was in the conference room, I said, "And this is Winslow's brother, Carl."

A round of hellos and waves followed as I ushered Winslow a few more steps into the conference room, then introduced the team. Once all of that was over, though, I was left standing there without any clue how to get out of the weird situation I'd caused.

"Why don't you two come in and join us," Nick said, standing with a smile and stepping to the side to fetch one of the spare chairs from the stack against the wall.

Everyone started to shift and make room at the table, but Winslow said, "Oh, God, I didn't mean to interrupt your meeting. We can go."

"No, honey," Nick said in that typically Nick way he had, "I don't think you can go right now. You're down here because of the bond, aren't you?"

Winslow swallowed, his Adam's apple bobbing guiltily, and nodded. The way he lowered his head tore through me and made me want to roar and fight the invisible demons that put a sad look like that on my omega's face.

Unfortunately, that caused Garrett to say, "Oh. I see. Yeah, we might have a bit of a problem."

I didn't know whether I wanted to punch him or feel grateful that someone else finally caught onto the hitch in the situation.

"Every problem has a solution," Phillip said, sounding just like his dad as he got up to add a chair for Carl to the table.

"Well, the obvious solution," Sal said, still unmoved from his spot at the head of the table, "is that Ty needs to take Winslow with him on the trip to Norwalk."

Winslow was in the middle of sitting down, but he jerked like he would stand again. "Wouldn't I just get in the way?" he asked, finally settling into the chair, but sitting like the seat was lined with thumbtacks.

I reached for his hand under the table, both to reassure him and to calm myself.

"On the contrary," Nick said as he resumed his seat by Sal's side. "I have a feeling you might be of great help to Ty on this trip."

"Oh, Winslow is super helpful," Carl said, shifting around in his chair as though he were thrilled to be at a board meeting, and like he fancied himself important because of it. "He's always pitching in and lending a helping hand whenever someone needs something. He fed Mrs. McCready's cat and emptied the litter box every day when she went to visit her niece for a month, even though she didn't pay him. If Winslow has any sort of fault at all, it's that he never asks for money for—"

"I don't think Winslow will be a problem on this trip," I said cutting Carl off. I really hoped I wouldn't have to continue on with the second half of that thought, and that looking at Carl after the speech he'd made would be enough to signal to the others what the bigger problem was.

Blessedly, Nick—ever the perceptive one—said, "I'm certain we could find something for Carl to do around the mountain while you and Winslow are in Norwalk."

"Me?" Carl looked shocked to be considered in the discussion at all. "I mean, I guess I could do something. I could also go with Winslow. We're sort of a team like that."

I clenched my jaw, staring straight down at the top of the table. It was bad enough that I suddenly had a million things to sort out in my personal life, but having those things come up in a meeting with my colleagues was borderline too much for me to swallow. Already, I wouldn't trade Winslow for the world, but the situation was unprofessional.

It wasn't just that I couldn't be an ESA anymore, it was that my whole image as the guy who had everything under control, who could handle any situation with aplomb, was shot to shit. I was spiraling, and I knew it would change the way my colleagues saw me. I hated it.

"Winslow, would you like your brother to accompany you on this trip?" Sal asked.

The question shocked me and Winslow both. Winslow's hand tightened around mine before he let go entirely and folded his hands on the tabletop.

"Um," he said, peeking at Carl in the seat next to him, then bit his lip for a half-second. "I don't want either of us to be a burden. I don't mind helping out in any way I can, and if you have something for Carl to do, that would be good."

My mouth twitched into the beginning of a smile before I steadied my reaction. With an answer like that, Winslow could be a diplomat. He wanted Carl to stand on his own two feet, but he didn't want to hurt his brother by telling him as much, especially not in front of a conference room filled with strangers. I didn't need the bond to tell me that much. It fit with everything I'd come to know about my omega in the last few days.

Winslow was a good man. Maybe better than I deserved.

"It's settled, then," Nick said with a smile for Carl. "Carl will stay here and help Joe out with a few things in the office, or Hannah in Landscaping, if she needs an extra set of hands. We'll figure out exactly where you will be most useful."

"And I'm certain Winslow would be most useful by Ty's side, wooing clients," Sal said, as if that were the end of that.

I noted the way Winslow flinched a little about the implied job Sal had given him. I could still feel the crushing uncertainty from last night through the bond. But the plus side was that if just the two of us made the trip to Norwalk, it would provide us with all the time we needed to talk things through.

And we desperately needed that time. Just because bonding only happened between two people who were inherently compatible to begin with didn't mean there wasn't anything to talk about. I felt in my body and soul that Winslow and I belonged together somehow, but it would take a lot of talking and a lot of work to figure out where we as a couple fit in with the rest of the world.

Chapter Thirteen

Winslow

I didn't know new lives happened that fast, but by the time Ty and I—and Carl—walked out of the meeting, I was well aware that I'd stepped into a whole new life, and that I was there to stay.

The problem was, it felt like I'd put on someone else's shoes and clothes and was attempting to get away with pretending to be them. I followed Ty around the Bangers & Mash office, sort of helping him gather what looked like marketing materials for the people in Norwalk we would be going to see—while Carl got in the way, peeking in closets, searching through drawers, and being told every ten minutes not to mess with things that weren't his. It was really nice of Mr. Banger and Mr. Mash to let me walk around like I belonged on their mountain, and even nicer for them to rope Carl into helping fix an awning of some sort that had broken on the building that housed a cafeteria.

I was much more comfortable in the afternoon, once Ty took me back to the cabin so we could do laundry and pack for the trip. Carl was still helping with the awning, so it was just the two of us, which was a relief. But I still didn't really feel like talking about things, even though I could sense Ty wanted me to talk.

Honestly, I was impressed with how patient Ty was, particularly for an alpha. I'd always been told alphas were aggressive and demanding, and that if they wanted something, particularly from an omega like me, they would just take it. Kind of like my father had been with my mom...until he walked out entirely when I was four. But Ty was different. He let me keep my thoughts to myself so I could mull everything over and decide what I felt. Even when we went to bed that night.

That was another thing. Ty didn't put any sort of moves on me. I was certain that he would. One night of him not trying to get in my pajama pants could be explained away by heat exhaustion. Two? Well, maybe those things I'd heard about alphas being oversexed was wrong too.

All of that—Ty turning out to be super nice, him not forcing me to talk and not pushing me to have sex—seemed to help the rest of the weirdness of suddenly being bonded to someone I didn't know calm down. It also helped that I slept like a log again that night. And by the time I woke up the next morning, draped all over Ty once again, my morning wood pressed against his side, his morning-hard cock hot against my thigh, I was actually starting to feel settled about things.

I blinked and stretched to wake myself up more, began to pull away from Ty, then realized I didn't want to. Instead, I snuggled closer to him, breathed in his forest rain scent, and let myself consider, even if it was just for a moment, that maybe this was where I was supposed to be.

"Morning, baby," Ty murmured, shifting a little so he could kiss the top of my head.

I moved so that I could prop myself on one arm beside him, still half draped over him, but able to look at him.

"I've always hated pet names or people talking to me like I'm a kid," I said. Ty's hazy, contented smile started to drop, so I rushed on with, "But somehow I don't mind it at all when you talk to me that way."

Ty's smile came back, but it had lost some of its laziness. He reached up and swept his hand across my face and hair, which I'd noticed he liked to touch. "Could be the hormones," he said. "Could be the bond."

I shrugged one shoulder. "That's probably it."

I suddenly wanted to talk about everything that I'd been too confused to deal with the day before—the bond, what it meant for the two of us, how I'd ruined his career, and what we were supposed to do next to pick up the pieces of everything I'd broken. I even opened my mouth to start the conversation. But a crash in the kitchen ended any hope I might have had about sorting things out.

"Carl," I sighed, rolling over and throwing back the covers with the force of my irritation.

"Can't he take care of himself?" Ty asked, getting out of bed a little slower.

I laughed ironically, heading straight for the door, even though I needed to pee. "I'm afraid of what would happen if he tried," I said.

Only when I made it out to the hall and halfway to the kitchen did it dawn on me that Ty's question might actually have been a plea for me to just stay in bed with him and talk instead of rushing to Carl's rescue.

Carl needed rescue, though. He'd dropped a glass in the kitchen while in bare feet, and when I got there, he was trying to pick up shards of glass without moving his feet. As soon as I stepped into the room, he glanced up at me and blurted, "It wasn't me, I swear. The glass was wet when I picked it up."

I rolled my eyes and walked to the kitchen closet, careful to avoid the pieces of glass I could see, since I was in bare feet too.

"You need to be more careful, Carl," I said as I pulled out a broom and dustpan I'd seen in there the day before.

I wanted to add, "I can't take care of you forever," in the wake of what Ty had asked minutes before, but for some reason, just thinking that hurt too much. Mom needed me to look after Carl.

"Winslow, come away from there," Ty said, appearing in the kitchen doorway a second later. "You'll cut your feet."

I couldn't argue with that, so I handed the broom and dustpan over to him—he was the smart one and had put slippers on before stepping into the kitchen—then headed off to the bathroom to pee and clean up.

It was a rocky start to the morning, which was depressing. Ty and I had been so close to figuring out a little more about what was going on with us. I told myself it was okay, there would be other opportunities, we had plenty of time together. That carried me through cleaning up and getting dressed, then joining Ty and Carl in the kitchen, where breakfast was already in progress.

Since Ty and I needed to get out on the road as soon as possible, breakfast was just cereal, toast, and coffee, but I really didn't mind.

"There needs to be some sort of system for sweeping up broken glass from hard floors," Carl chattered away as we all ate. "Like one of those automatic vacuum robot things for carpets, but that picks up glass instead of dirt. I wonder what it would take to invent something like that. I bet it would make a ton of money."

"I'm sure it would," I said absently, studying Ty over the lip of my coffee mug.

We had to talk about things. He wanted to. I wanted to. Well, I wanted to, but I was a little scared of where the conversation would go. Was I just another dowdy house-omega now? Would I end up with nothing to do but keep the house clean, eat too many carbs, and watch trash TV all day?

That might have been Carl's goal in life—although, really, I was certain even Carl wanted to do useful things with his life, especially since he finished breakfast first, then headed out, saying they needed his help in the office—but it definitely wasn't mine. I needed to do something productive with my time, but was I even allowed to do that now?

"Let's finish packing and get the truck loaded up," Ty said as we cleaned up breakfast and headed out of the kitchen.

"I'm glad we did laundry yesterday," I said as I followed him into the bedroom. "I don't have a lot of clothes. How long will we be gone again?"

"Just a couple of days," Ty said with a smile as he pulled what looked like an overnight bag out of his closet. "And if you need more clothes, I'm more than happy to buy them for you."

I squirmed a little at that statement, as kind as it was, and started pulling some of my clothes from the drawer Ty had given me to keep them in. Ty headed into the bathroom to shower and change, and I finished packing both of our things into the one bag as he did, but the way his statement lingered in the air was the perfect opportunity to start up the necessary conversation once he came out again.

"So, I know I should feel fine about you buying a bunch of new clothes for me, since you have a job and money and I don't," I said, feeling so awkward, but pushing myself to get it out there anyhow, "but it feels like I'm taking advantage of you."

Ty let out a breath, like he was relieved I'd finally said something.

"Winslow, you don't need to feel awkward about this," he said, coming over to the bed and checking everything I'd packed. He'd evidently packed up all the toiletries after his shower and added a travel bag of those things to the overnight bag, then zipped it up. "What happened, happened, and it's definitely going to be a good thing."

I wanted to believe him, but as he hefted the bag over his shoulder and gestured for me to head out to the main room, then outside to where his truck was parked, I continued to wince and squirm and wonder.

"I'm used to taking care of people, not being taken care of," I said, considering myself really brave for blurting something like that to a man who, biologically and socially, was expected to take care of me now. "I never imagined anything like this happening, and it's like I've been hired for a job that I don't know how to do."

Since the overnight bag wasn't really that big, Ty brought it with him into the cab as we climbed into the truck, tucking it in the space between the seat and the back window instead of storing it in the truck bed.

"Honestly, I never imagined this happening to me either," he said as he turned the ignition, then backed the truck out, then got us on our way. "And even if I did hope to find a mate someday, this is not the way I thought it would happen."

He sent me a sideways look that had a little humor in it. I could deal with that. It was nice that he was attempting to lighten the mood when we had such serious things to talk about.

"Did you ever see yourself getting married and...having a family?" I asked, hesitating on that last part. I barely felt ready to talk about being bonded, let alone having Ty's babies. My stomach went all weird at the idea...but maybe not in a bad way.

Ty sent me a sideways smile before focusing on the road. "I

think I did always imagine myself with an omega and a family someday," he said.

"You think?" That wasn't as reassuring as I wanted it to be.

Ty's face grew serious again, and I kind of knew what he was going to say before he said it, "I imagined my career as an ESA would go on for another ten years or so."

That statement brought up a ton of guilt in me.

"I'm sorry," I said, leaning my elbow against the edge of the window and rubbing my forehead. "I ruined your career and your life."

"You changed it," Ty said, sounding like he was irritated with me. "It's not ruined yet."

I didn't know whether to smile or groan at the "yet" part.

I was about to throw up another round of apologies, but Ty cut that off by asking, "What did you envision your life being like? Did *you* ever think you'd get married and have a family?"

My eyes went wide and my brow flew up. "Is that a sort of proposal?"

Ty laughed. The sound was like pouring liquid comfort down my spine and letting it pool in my groin.

"Let's deal with one thing at a time," he said, sneaking another sideways smile at me. "Although, since we're bonded, it might be inevitable."

I was smiling before I knew what came over me—which had to be the bond—but then that smile dropped.

"Bonds can be broken, though, can't they?" I asked.

Ty grew serious as well. "In theory, yes. But I've never heard of a case of any couple deliberately breaking their bond." He stole another look before turning onto the highway at the bottom of the mountain. "Bonds happen for a reason, and Nick said yesterday, they only happen when people are inherently compatible. So why break that?"

I made a sound and shrugged, then looked out the window at the passing trees that skirted the bottom of the mountain, forming a narrow barrier between the private property and Barrington's suburbs.

"I have always imagined I'd get married and have kids," I confessed, still looking out the window. "I just didn't plan to do it when I was barely twenty."

Ty glanced my way, then, because the road demanded his attention, he reached one hand out to touch my leg without looking at me.

It was probably instinct and biology that made me do it, but I reached for Ty's hand and held it on the seat between us.

"I never really figured out what I want to do with the rest of my life," I said. It was so much easier to talk about these things when I was touching Ty. And when it was just the two of us in an enclosed space.

"What did you study in college?" Ty asked.

I squirmed with discomfort. "I never even applied to college," I mumbled. "There wasn't time, since Mom dying during my senior year in high school meant I missed all the application deadlines. I wouldn't have been able to afford college anyhow. Carl and I were on our own before I graduated. We had to keep a roof over our heads and pay off some lingering stuff having to do with her care."

"I'm sorry," Ty said, squeezing my hand. Although he had to let go a second later to maneuver through some traffic. "And you two don't have any other family to help out?"

I shook my head. "Not really. Our dad left when we were kids, and his family has never really wanted anything to do with us. And Mom was an only child. My Grandpa is still alive, but he's in a home and can barely take care of himself."

I felt a strong wave of protectiveness from Ty, along with pinches of sadness and compassion. It actually felt nice, kind of like he was still holding my hand. Maybe this whole bond thing wasn't so bad after all. It made me feel like I wasn't totally alone in the world.

"What would you have studied if you'd been able to go to college?" Ty asked after getting around a slow spot of traffic.

"That's the thing," I said, sitting straighter and rolling my shoulders. "I don't know. I mean, I was good at English and History in school, but those aren't really careers. Mom was sick all through high school, so while the other people in my class were hatching plans to be doctors or lawyers or astrophysicists, I was driving her to chemo appointments or helping pay the bills when she was too tired." I shrugged again. "Maybe I'd be good at some sort of nursing or caretaking job, like Carl said?"

Ty glanced my way. "Is that what you want to do?"

"Not really," I sighed. "But that just takes me back in a circle, because I don't know what I want to do."

To my surprise, Ty smiled, and it filled me with a sense of tenderness. "Sounds to me like what you really need is some time to rest."

I laughed out loud at that. "I will never get time to rest as long as Carl needs me."

I intended the statement to be lighthearted, but I felt a twinge of anger through the bond.

"It's not like that," I said, as if he'd made a verbal comment. "Carl is my brother. I love him. You've seen what he can do when he isn't being supervised."

Ty grunted and gripped the steering wheel tighter.

"He can't really hold down a job," I went on with a sigh. "Like I said the other day, we never had him tested, but there are probably reasons why he can't focus and why he gets into trouble. He's not mentally deficient or anything, though."

"Your brother is not your responsibility," Ty said, and I could tell he was trying to be careful with his words. "He's not your life. You deserve to have your own life."

I knew he was trying to be nice, but those words made me feel worse.

"I'm not so sure about that," I said, leaning against the window again. "Do I really deserve my own life when I've gone and ruined yours?"

A different sort of burst of frustration vibrated through the bond.

"I'm not your responsibility either, Winslow," Ty said.

"Because I'm yours now?" I suggested, one eyebrow raised.

I could tell I'd caught him there. A pulse of sheepishness passed through the bond that only seemed to highlight the underlying possessiveness that had been a constant from Ty since the bond had formed.

"How about we say we're responsible for each other?" Ty suggested. I could tell he was trying to smile again, for my sake.

"Okay, but I still feel bad for being such a burden to you," I said. "And don't go telling me I'm not a burden," I cut him off when I saw and felt he was going to protest. "You didn't ask for me. I've legitimately made a mess of your career. And bond or no bond, we're only just getting to know each other. Relationships always mean work."

Ty surprised me again by smiling when I thought he would be angry. I even felt a rush of happiness and...admiration through the bond.

"I like that you're so blunt and pragmatic," he said, turning his head to flash his smile directly at me. "Those aren't typical omega traits."

"I guess this is where I say I'm not your typical omega," I said, actually smiling back at him.

"You aren't," Ty said with a nod. "And I like that. Don't feel bad about everything that's happened. Nature isn't stupid. I think we'll make a really good team, once this initial craziness sorts itself out."

"You really think so?" Hope flared in me so fast it made

me breathless. I hadn't thought to consider that Ty and I might actually work out. We could even turn into one of those super sweet old couples that drove their grandkids up a wall with how cutesy they were.

That thought was so weird and felt so big that I sucked in a breath and sat straighter.

"Who knows?" Ty shrugged, the feeling coming from him softening and turning more comfortable. "This is just the beginning, right? Anything could happen."

"I guess so," I said, maybe allowing myself to consider that.

"So, assuming everything is going to work out fine," Ty said, "what would you want to do with the rest of your life? Because if you want to go to college, I'm totally on board with that. And if you want to start a family—"

I felt a hot, electric burst of emotion from him that was too big and too confused to interpret, but that somehow, bizarrely, made my womb tighten. I absolutely should not have been able to feel something like that, but having just gone through heat, I was more aware of my anatomy than ever before.

I opened my mouth to reply, but before words could make it out, there was a loud tapping on the back window that shocked me out of my skin. Especially since we were going eighty miles an hour on the highway.

It alarmed Ty as well, I could tell—through the bond and because he swerved slightly when he looked in the rearview mirror. He hissed a curse under his breath.

I twisted with a jerk when the tapping came again, and then I swore way louder than under my breath.

"Carl! What the fuck?" I yelled, glaring at my brother as he pressed himself against the back window from the truck's bed.

Chapter Fourteen

Ty

I was going to kill him. I was going to wring Carl's scrawny little beta neck, whether he was Winslow's brother or not.

That thought was immediately followed by a much deeper worry that Carl really would get himself killed because he'd stowed away in the back of the truck. I should have checked under the tarp in the back before setting out for Norwalk.

I eased up on the gas, signaled, and moved over to the right and onto the shoulder as carefully as I could, glad there wasn't too much traffic on the highway yet.

"Fuck, Carl!" Winslow shouted through the window again. "Are you trying to get yourself killed?"

"I'll get him," I said, probably sounding like I would get Carl and drag him to the nearest hangman's noose, as I brought the truck to a full stop and cut the engine. "Stay in the truck."

That last order was probably unnecessary, but if Winslow

tried to climb out of the truck to help his brother in the middle of traffic and ended up struck by a morning commuter, I really would wring Carl's neck.

"Wow! I didn't think that would be as hair-raising as all that," Carl said, already climbing out of the truck's bed on the driver's side. "I wasn't going to come out until we got to Norwalk, but it's way uncomfortable to bump around in the back of a truck on the highway."

As soon as the wiry beta landed on the gravel at the edge of the shoulder, I grabbed the front of his shirt and pulled him closer to me.

"You listen to me, Carl," I said as low as I could and still be heard over the rush of cars. "You were supposed to stay at the institute. Winslow is exhausted from taking care of you, and your mother too, and he needs a break." I was certain of that after our conversation. My omega had been forced to handle far too much for a man his age, and it was getting to him, whether he recognized it or not. "Now, we're getting in the truck, we're turning around, and I'm taking you back to the mountain, where you will behave yourself for—"

"No," Winslow's gloomy voice said from only a few feet away from me.

I snapped straight and let go of Carl's shirt—that was an overreaction on my part anyhow, and I felt foolish for it the second I saw the hopelessness in Winslow's eyes—and turned to Winslow.

"He'll just get into more trouble if we take him back and leave him unsupervised," Winslow said, rubbing above his right eye, as if he had a headache.

"Hey, I'm right here," Carl said with a scowl. "And I'm not some hyper toddler who needs a babysitter." He glanced between me and Winslow, then let his shoulders drop. "I've never been to Norwalk, okay? I've never been anywhere outside of Barrington. I just really wanted to go and you...you didn't even ask me if I wanted to come along."

I scowled. Whether Carl was faking it or not, his hangdog expression and sob story weren't going to affect me.

They totally affected Winslow. I could feel it even before I turned to him with a questioning look, to see what he wanted to do.

"Fine," Winslow said, throwing up his hands. "You can come to Norwalk. But Ty is going for business, not for sightseeing, so you can't cause trouble or get in the way, okay?"

"I'll be as quiet as a mouse," Carl said, breaking into a smile and striding for the truck door. "You won't even know I'm there," he added, climbing in on the driver's side, then scooting all the way to the far end to the passenger's seat. "Oh, wow! Did you see that Corvette that just zipped by?"

I forced myself to take a deep, calming breath. This was not the trip I'd hoped to have.

Then again, nothing for the past week had turned out the way I'd expected it to.

"I'm really sorry," Winslow said, taking a step closer to me. "I should have known better. I should have made absolutely certain Carl wasn't in the truck before we left."

"Your brother is not your responsibility," I repeated what I'd said earlier, even though I'd thought the same thing about checking the truck.

"Yeah, but he kind of is, and now you can see why," Winslow said. He shoved his hands in his jeans pockets and stared down at the gravel.

It hurt. It physically hurt to see my omega sucked back onto the treadmill that I suspected more and more he'd been on for years.

I moved closer to him and put a hand on his shoulder. That immediately elicited a warm response through our bond.

"We'll deal with it," I said. "And hey, at least this way, I'll get to sit closer to you for the rest of the trip, which is especially nice, since you seem to have recovered from your heat."

Winslow sent me the most devastating, shy smile. "Yeah, there's that."

I smiled in return. "Come on," I said, turning him and nudging him toward the open truck door. I really wanted to smack that pert ass of his, just to be funny, but we weren't anywhere near that point yet.

Winslow climbed into the truck and slid into the middle seat, reaching for the seatbelt right away. I got in after him, buckled up, and started the engine again.

"Norwalk is on a river, right?" Carl started talking even before I'd pulled back onto the highway. "I remember seeing it on maps as a kid. It's one of those mid-sized cities that people are always saying are up and coming, but they just seem to stay mid-sized. I think that has something to do with the shift in industry away from manufacturing and into the service industry, or something like that. A lot of those kinds of cities were built along waterways, because it was easier to transport stuff by water instead of over land back in the day."

I peeked sideways at Winslow once we were driving steadily along in the flow of traffic. Winslow returned my look with a gloomy expression of apology as Carl launched into a story about some guy he knew online who lived in Greenville, another mid-sized city out on the West Coast.

I tried not to be one of those gruff, glowering alphas without any patience, but the drive to Norwalk was three hours long, and Carl's surprise presence had smashed what had been the first real, honest conversation Winslow and I had had. I couldn't stop thinking about the few things we'd been able to discuss in that time, even though that meant leaving Winslow to field the bulk of Carl's chattering throughout the drive.

Winslow had been floundering before we met. He'd just

lost his job, and although he didn't specify why or how, I just knew Carl had something to do with that. Possibly it was the bicycle thing, which made Winslow late for work. Winslow had implied he'd had trouble keeping jobs because of Carl. I hadn't had a clue what that meant at first, but now I wondered if Carl had a history of showing up in Winslow's business, literally and figuratively, and sucking all the energy out of him.

If I had to guess, I'd've said that all started when the two of them were dealing with their mother's illness and death. I'd never gone through anything like that, since both of my dads were still alive and healthy, but I knew from studying psychology that things like that profoundly affected people, especially young people who were asked to take on more than they should. If I had to put money on it, I would have said that Winslow was dealing with the whole thing by extending his caretaker role, and Carl had issues with separating from his brother, the only family he had left.

Of course, analyzing it like an armchair grief counselor didn't do a damn thing to fix the situation, or even to give me a clue how it might be fixed. Therapy, yes, but not in the middle of a business trip.

"Holy crap! When you said we were going on a business trip, I imagined another office building, like the ones up on that mountain," Carl exclaimed, leaning forward to gawp out the windshield as I made the turn my GPS told me to, onto the driveway of Kevin Sanchez and Madeline Cross's estate. "This is like...like a mansion or something."

"It is, indeed, a mansion," I said with as much patience as I could manage, which wasn't a lot. "The clients, Sanchez and Cross, are philanthropists. He inherited money, and she started a successful real estate business, then sold it for a huge profit. They're passionate about omega rights, and they're working in partnership with the government of Norwalk to bring a Bangers & Mash branch to the city so that omegas here can have access to safe and discreet heat support services."

My explanation was for Winslow. He probably knew as much already from sitting in on the meeting the day before, but it felt good to explain it to him in a way that emphasized helping omegas like him. I was rewarded with a nod from Winslow and a general feeling of positivity through our bond.

"Man, I wish I was an alpha," Carl said, still sucked in by the house and its grounds as I drove up to park in what I hoped was a convenient spot beside a couple other, fancier cars. "I could be an ESA and make a ton of money at the same time."

I sent Carl a flat, sideways look as I cut the engine, then reached to undo my seatbelt. As it happened, I caught Winslow's eyes. He returned my flat look, as if to say there was no way in hell Carl would ever be accepted into ESA training.

That moment actually made me smile. It was a connection, albeit a brief one and one that came at the expense of someone else. But at that point, I was willing to take any chance to connect with my omega that I could get.

"Oh my gosh, I think that shrub is shaped like a fish," Carl said, practically leaping out the passenger door. "I love topiaries."

"Maybe we should put him on a leash," Winslow sighed as he scooted toward the passenger door.

"He's just happy to be going on an adventure," I said, trying really hard to give Carl the benefit of the doubt.

Two minutes later, as we made our way up to the front door, I wondered if a leash would have been a good idea after all.

"Carl, come on," Winslow called to him as Carl leaned into one of the sports cars, cupping his hands around the sides of his face so he could peer at the interior. "It's rude to look into people's cars like that."

"But it's a Porsche! You should see the interior of this thing, though," Carl said as he tore himself away from the car, just as the front door opened. "I've never seen leather like that. These people must be super rich."

I'd had video chats with both Sanchez and Cross, so I knew it was Sanchez himself and not a butler or staff member who opened the front door right as Carl made his comment. It was absolutely not the way I wanted the trip to start off.

Especially since Sanchez didn't laugh at Carl's comment and brush the whole thing off like I hoped he would.

"Mr. Martin," Sanchez said, blinking a few times, watching Carl as if he might break into the Porsche, then looking at me again. "We've been expecting you."

There was just enough of a hint in Sanchez's voice that he was not expecting anyone *but* me to make me worry.

"Mr. Sanchez. It's good to finally meet in person," I said, extending a hand to him, alpha to alpha. As soon as Sanchez shook it and let go, I rested a hand on the small of Winslow's back and said, "This is my omega, Winslow Grant."

The introduction was purely to dig myself out of the hole of bringing two uninvited guests with me on the trip, but it felt damned good to introduce Winslow as mine.

Better still, Sanchez's expression softened into a smile. "It's a pleasure to meet you, Mr. Grant," he said, offering Winslow his hand. As Winslow shook it, Sanchez looked back to me. "I didn't know you had such a handsome mate. I was under the impression that you were single, that you worked as an ESA yourself."

"It's a relatively new situation," I said.

I intended to say more, but Carl stepped up between me and Winslow, thrust out his hand to Sanchez, and said, "Ty found Winslow in a hotel lobby last week in the middle of heat. He thought Winslow was his client, which, of course, he wasn't, because we don't have that kind of money, but Ty didn't know that and took him upstairs to have wild heat sex anyhow." And if that wasn't bad enough, he added, "It was my brother's first time, and for some reason, they bonded."

I should have left Carl on the side of the road.

"Oh. I see." Sanchez shook Carl's hand gingerly, then took a step back. "Do come in."

Carl stepped right into the house, without any sense that maybe I should have gone first, since I was the only expected guest, not to mention the one who was there to do business with our hosts. At least it meant Carl stepped out from between me and Winslow, which allowed me to sway closer to Winslow as we joined Sanchez and Carl in a massive hall.

"These people are rich," Winslow whispered so that only I could hear.

I could feel his anxiety like it was hot wax he'd spilled on me, and not in the good way. My instinct was to take his hand, but that gesture would have been just a hair too infantilizing. I wanted Winslow to feel confident, like he had in the truck at the very beginning of our conversation. Sanchez had responded warmly to Winslow as my omega, and instinct told me we could use that to seal the deal for a B&M branch.

"Has our guest arrived?" The question was accompanied by the click of heels on the hall's marble floor as Madeline Cross walked in from the hallway off to one side.

She stopped and blinked with the same look of surprise at the sight of three people where she'd expected one.

"Maddy, you know Tybalt Martin from our chats," Sanchez said, making the introductions as Cross came to stand beside him. "And this is Mr. Martin's omega, Winslow Grant." Cross glanced to Winslow with a delighted smile. "But I have yet to be properly introduced to Mr....?"

"Grant," I said, praying there was a way I could make everything right. "Carl Grant. Winslow's brother. I apologize for not giving you advanced notice that I wouldn't be traveling alone. It came as a bit of a surprise to me too. Carl is staying with me and Winslow for the time being."

I sent Carl a look that all but demanded he straighten up and fly right.

"I'm kind of a stowaway," Carl said, somehow, blessedly, managing to look charming instead of like the nuisance he was. "You're gorgeous, you know," he told Cross with a starry-eyed look, making me second-guess the slack I'd been willing to cut him.

"Well," Cross laughed. "Thank you very much. You're not so bad yourself." She nudged Sanchez, maybe rubbing it in that someone had given her a compliment, then clapped her hands together. "Welcome to our humble home. You're just in time for lunch. But how about a quick tour of the place first, then we can start swapping ideas about the possible partnership between Bangers & Mash and Norwalk."

I was relieved that neither Sanchez nor Cross had us thrown out for bad behavior. More than that, I was actually glad to have Winslow with me as we were given a quick tour of the house and its gardens. Cross was an omega, but she was also a dynamo. I knew from the conversations we'd had so far that hers was the energy fueling this project. It was unusual for an omega to have made such a name for themselves without their alpha, even in this day and age, and I wanted Winslow to see that the sky truly was the limit, if he could just lose the things holding him down and reach for the stars.

Unfortunately, one of those things holding him down followed us around the estate, making inappropriate comments the entire time.

"It must be nice to inherit an entire fortune from your parents," he said offhandedly to Sanchez as the tour ended in a perfectly landscaped garden that looked out over the river, where white wicker furniture had been set up with an amazing lunch spread.

Sanchez stared back at him, clearly insulted. "My family has worked hard to build a name for ourselves for generations," he said.

"Yeah, but it must be nice to get such a great head start in life," Carl pressed on. "Winslow and I barely had anything, but we work hard too. The best we've gotten is Winslow accidentally bonding with a great guy like Ty."

I could feel Winslow's embarrassment and panic through the bond. Carl just didn't know when to quit.

"From what I've seen so far and from my research, Norwalk would be the perfect place for a Bangers & Mash branch," I said, pretending to be casual as we were all seated around the table.

Fortunately, Carl was seated on one side of me with Winslow on the other, and when Carl opened his mouth to make another comment, I kicked his shin hard.

There was no guarantee that doing something so juvenile would actually work, but surprisingly, Carl kept his mouth shut as Cross said, "Norwalk hasn't had the same concentration of alphas and omegas as some of the larger cities have, since the town was originally founded by betas, who saw the location as ideal for industry. But as the demographics of the city have changed, the need for omega services has increased, and it's been hard to keep up with demands."

"Are there any omega services in Norwalk?" Winslow asked. He was a bit timider than I would have liked him to be, but I was pleased that he'd apparently asked the right question at the right time.

"We've been getting better at public services of all kinds," Sanchez said as a staff member brought heaping bowls of colorful salad to the table. "Sanchez-Cross Enterprises has just started a program of building affordable housing for underserved members of the community, for example."

"Oh, like those people who go in and build houses for

poor people after floods and things?" Carl asked, his eyes alight with too much interest.

So much for keeping a lid on him.

Sanchez smiled tightly at him. "Yes, like that."

"We could give you a tour of some of the neighborhoods we've been working on tomorrow, along with the rest of the tour we have planned," Cross said. "Maybe there's a way to integrate a Bangers & Mash office with some of the housing developments we're working on."

"I'd like to see that," Carl said, as if he were the one running the show.

Sanchez went stiff at the comment, but Cross was still charmed by Carl. "We'll definitely do it, then," she said. "Now, you have to try these salads. They were made completely with produce from the hydroponic gardens we've been experimenting with. My thought is that we could equip some of these new neighborhoods with hydroponic gardens as a way to prevent food deserts in less-advantaged parts of Norwalk."

We all picked up our forks, and I did my best to smile and focus politely on business. But if I were honest with myself, it felt like I had a time-bomb on one side with Carl and an enigma on the other with Winslow. It was a business trip, but with every breath I took and everything around me, I wanted to find ways to make Winslow feel at ease, important, and happy with the twist of fate that had brought us together.

It was a definite change from spending ten years with laser-like focus on my career.

And I still didn't have a clue what to do about it.

Chapter Fifteen

Winslow

I'd come so close to psyching myself up and deciding that I would do everything in my power to make Ty's business trip a success. Even if I had to lock Carl in a closet and lean against the door to keep him from getting out while Ty sealed his deal for Bangers & Mash, I would. I owed it to Ty, owed it to him not to be an anchor that would bring his career prospects down. And I'd convinced myself that I would actually be able to do it too.

Right up until Mr. Sanchez pulled open his front door and frowned at us.

I hadn't realized we would be dealing with *really* rich people. I don't know why I didn't make that connection sooner, since people with enough money to finance something like an emergency heat support place generally had to be *really* rich to do it. But it hadn't dawned on me that we would be staying in a mansion, eating incredibly fancy food, and attempting to sell an idea to people who wore designer clothes, didn't have a hair out of place, and who drove sports cars.

I was wearing jeans and old sneakers that were getting a hole near one toe, and I definitely needed a haircut. And Ty thought I would be able to *help* his cause?

This was never going to work.

The best I could do was to try not to touch anything as we went on a tour of the mansion and its gardens—I was definitely not from the kind of stock who knew how to exist in the sort of surroundings I found myself in—and to eat everything I was served at lunch, and later dinner, without complaining. Even when I wasn't exactly sure what was swimming in the rich cream sauce at dinner.

Ironically, Carl either didn't seem to notice that we were way out-classed by Mr. Sanchez and Mrs. Cross or he didn't care.

"...and somehow we got away with it," he said with a laugh, finishing up a story about how the two of us had broken into the kitchen at summer camp when I was twelve and Carl was thirteen to "liberate" a bunch of ice cream sandwiches for the other campers.

Well, Carl had broken in. I had been dragged along and spent the whole time trying desperately to keep us from getting caught.

"You should have seen the looks on the faces of the other campers," Carl went on, sliding his fork through the seven-layer chocolate cake we'd been served for dessert. "So, in a way," he said after taking a bite, his mouth still full, "I have experience in philanthropy too."

Mrs. Cross laughed at Carl's story, which was a relief, but Mr. Sanchez frowned at Carl, clearly impatient with the loud-mouth beta who had crashed his nice little business meeting.

"I have a few people I should introduce you to," Mrs. Cross told Carl, apparently oblivious to what a wreck he was.

She glanced across the table to her husband and said, "Don't you think Harrison would just love Carl?"

"Perhaps," Mr. Sanchez said icily.

I choked down another bite of cake, not really wanting it. My stomach was in knots as I waited for whatever embarrassing thing Carl would do next.

Under the table, Ty put a hand on my thigh. The gesture was meant to comfort me, I was sure, but it made me jump a little instead. Not enough to draw attention, but it sent my heart racing and my stomach churning, and after that, there was no way I could finish my cake.

Fortunately, it seemed like dinner was over anyhow.

"We should make an early night of it," Mr. Sanchez said, pushing his chair back and standing. "We have a lot of business to discuss in the morning."

As soon as he rose, the rest of us stood as well—even Carl, though he wasn't finished eating his cake and shoveled the last few mouthfuls in while he stood. It reminded me of all those historical TV shows where everyone rose when the king rose or they risked getting their heads cut off. Mr. Sanchez definitely gave me the "heads will roll" vibe.

Which only made me feel more like I was ruining Ty's one shot to do his job and help omegas. It hadn't even occurred to me that the deal he was there to seal might fall through, but while everyone made small talk as we left the dining room and Ty and I started upstairs to the guestroom we'd been given, I was beginning to see that failure was a real possibility.

"I don't know about you, but I'm exhausted," Ty said as he closed the door behind us and headed toward the massive bed with its carved posts and soft, blue bedcovers. "Why don't you use the bathroom first."

I nodded without saying anything, grabbed my pajamas from the top of the dresser, where I'd unpacked them earlier, and headed to the bathroom. I could feel Ty's concern through the bond, and I felt horrible for giving him reasons to worry. I didn't know what to say that could reassure him, though.

For a few minutes in the truck, when we'd first started out that morning, I'd believed that maybe this wasn't such a colossal mistake on the part of Mother Nature after all and that Ty and I really were compatible and could make a life together.

But now, as I brushed my teeth and stared at my scruffy reflection in the mirror, I doubted it again. It wasn't just that I'd crushed any possibility of Ty ever working as an ESA again, I was under-educated, poor, and totally beneath him. I didn't want to think it, but I couldn't shake the feeling that I was going to bring Ty down.

Maybe I could find a way out of this. Bonds could be broken, after all.

"You okay in here?" Ty asked, knocking on the open bathroom door, then walking in as I spit and rinsed. "You seem a little...."

I splashed a handful of water over my mouth to wipe away the last of the toothpaste and glanced at Ty through the mirror. He'd felt my emotions through our bond, and now he was worried about me. Great. One more way that I was taking his attention away from what he really wanted.

"I'm...okay," I said as Ty walked past me to the fancy closet where the toilet was located. That little room meant he could pee while I washed my face, and it wasn't like he was peeing in the same room as me.

"You don't...feel okay," Ty said as he flushed and came out of the room to wash his hands.

He looked at me in the mirror as he did, and as he reached for his own toothbrush and the paste with a frown.

Something about looking at him through a mirror made it easier for me to say what was really on my mind.

"Is there a way to, I dunno, make the bond a little less sometimes?" It felt way to shameful to admit I'd been thinking about breaking the bond entirely. "I...I feel like I'm distracting you with all the stuff you can feel about me, and you don't need that sort of distraction right now."

Ty's brow knit in thought as he brushed his teeth. It seemed to take him forever, probably because I was waiting for an answer that I felt like I really needed.

When he finally spit and rinsed and stood straight, looking directly at me instead of through the mirror, he said, "There are plenty of ways to dampen a bond, but I'm not sure that's what I want."

"It's not?" My brow flew up.

Ty smiled at me. "Pushing this down is not going to help either of us adapt and get used to each other," he said.

I half rolled my eyes and leaned against the bathroom counter, arms crossed. "How do people ever get used to this?" I muttered, staring at the tiled floor.

"Hey," Ty said, shifting to stand in front of me—which meant I was trapped against the counter, his feet planted on either side of mine—and slipped a hand under my chin to lift my face to him. "It's going to be okay."

Everything about his movement, his words, the sound of his voice, and his scent was like a scene in a romantic movie, and whether I wanted it to or not, it struck me to the core. Shivers of lust vibrated through me, and my cock definitely took notice.

I could feel the warmth of reciprocation radiating from Ty. "You were great today," he said, his smile feeling as potent as his touch. "You asked all the right questions at the right times, and you had some good insights."

"I hardly said anything," I argued, but my voice didn't have any force to it. "Mr. Sanchez doesn't like me."

Ty blinked in surprise. "Sanchez adored you."

I didn't think so, but I didn't really want to argue with Ty. Besides, not even Ty could make the case that Mr. Sanchez liked or approved of Carl, and I'd clearly been the reason Carl was along for the ride.

"I don't belong in this sort of environment, Ty," I said before I lost my nerve. "This is too fancy for me. I don't know anything about business. I never even went to college. And I look like a total mess instead of someone you need—"

Ty silenced me by sliding an arm around my back and dipping down to slant his mouth over mine.

The last thing I expected in the middle of listing all the reasons why I was a disaster was to be kissed so hard it knocked the breath out of me. I did not expect to be pulled into Ty's powerful, alpha body and caressed as though I were precious. And I really didn't expect that I would instantly be so turned on that every other thought would be blasted from my mind.

A soft moan of pleasure filled the air, and only after the fact did I realize it came from me. As soon as I heard it, I jerked back, shocked at myself for being such a hussy.

Ty laughed, seeming to glow with arousal and happiness. "What?" he asked in a teasing tone. "Can't I kiss my omega if I want to?"

Another wave of pleasure and prickles raced through me. My instinct was to argue with every part of his question, but I couldn't. I *was* his omega, no matter how it had happened, and he *did* have every right to kiss me.

"I mean, I can't exactly say no, can I?" I lowered my head.

Ty's emotions immediately shifted to alarm and upset.

"Hey." He tipped my face up to him again and rested his big hand on the side of my face. "You can *always* say no. Always. I will never force you into something you aren't ready for." He paused, shifted a bit, then went on with, "I feel like you need reminding that, while us bonding was a surprise and me finding you was an accident, it definitely isn't a mistake. I know it in my soul. We're both probably still feeling the heat hormones too, which could mean we're not thinking straight about things. And right now, it sounds like you need me to make you feel good. That's all I want to do."

I swallowed hard, gazing up at Ty's impossibly handsome face. Was I allowed to just have sex with a guy? When I wasn't even in heat?

Of course I was. That was a stupid question. People slept around all the time, whether they were married or bonded or in a relationship or not. It was no big deal.

Except, it was a big deal for me. I didn't do that sort of thing. I didn't have time, and I had never felt like the kind of person who people wanted that way.

But the way Ty looked at me, like I was better than the chocolate cake we'd just eaten, had my blood pounding through me and slick leaking from my ass.

"I...I don't know...." I couldn't form my thoughts into words, couldn't figure out how to ask Ty if it was okay for me to want him, even though I was ruining him.

He could have backed off and pulled the whole "giving me time to sort things out" thing. Instead, he lifted me from the waist and held me against him while slanting his mouth over mine again.

I wrapped my legs around his waist on instinct, but fuck, it felt good. His big, hard cock settled against my ass, and even with two layers of pajamas between us, I felt how hot and ready it was. My dick pressed against his belly, which felt great too. I threw my arms around his shoulders and kissed him back, forcing my worries away.

Ty carried me out of the bathroom and back to the bed. He'd pulled the covers down while I was brushing my teeth, revealing clean, white sheets that looked buttery soft. He wasted no time laying me across those sheets on my back, then moving so that he could tug the hem of my pajama pants down, sliding them right off.

"I'm not even in heat," I panted, wriggling out of my t-shirt as Ty took off the rest of his clothes.

Ty's deep, sultry laughter shot right through me, making slick drip from my hole. "You're allowed to have sex when you're not in heat, Winslow," he said, definitely still teasing me. "Especially with your alpha."

The undiluted possessiveness with which he said that, coupled with the sight of his naked, hard, gorgeous body looming over me fired up every instinct for submission I didn't know I had and more. Part of me maybe resented it a little, but most of me felt like it clicked into some sort of wild, needy, slutty state of being where I just wanted to be fucked until I was a puddle on the mattress.

Biology for the win.

The way Ty's hot gaze raked over me as I lay spread out on the bed for him told me he felt a corresponding instinct. So much that it was a little bit scary when he pushed my legs up and apart to expose my wet hole to those lust-hazed eyes of his. He could do anything he wanted to me and I would be helpless.

What he actually did was lower himself to rub his stubbly cheek against my inner thigh, then kiss his way up my tingling skin to nuzzle my balls and taint. I thought for sure he would go straight to sucking my cock, but instead, he slid his tongue down to my hole and licked up the slick that had escaped. The slight roughness of his tongue against my sensitive hole felt so good that I nearly arched off the bed with pleasure.

I wasn't even in heat, like I'd told him, but my body responded like I needed him or I would explode. Or maybe I wanted to explode, but I needed him to light the fuse. I knew omegas were way more sensitive in certain places than alphas or betas, but Ty was the first person to ever prove that to me as he thrust his tongue into me with slow, hungry strokes, making me whimper and squirm with pleasure.

"Fuck, I'm gonna come, I'm gonna come," I panted, gripping the sheets on either side of me.

Ty let out a wicked laugh that vibrated through me and continued to do dirty, dirty things with his tongue. Which was how I guessed he was deliberately trying to make me come. Omegas had, like, an orgasm a minute during heat, but I didn't know what would happen outside of heat, and I really didn't want the whole thing to end as soon as it had started.

Ty didn't give me much choice about that, though. He kept up his sexy assault, and even though I panted and whimpered and made sounds that might have been begging, he pushed on until my whole body tensed, I thrust my hips instinctively, and hot ropes of cum spilled across my belly. Without me even needing to touch myself. That wasn't usual for me, as an omega, but it was like my body wanted to perform for my alpha and give him everything he wanted.

"Beautiful," Ty growled, shifting over me, dragging his tongue up the underside of my still twitching dick, then licking my cum off my stomach. "So, so beautiful."

The move was so erotic that my balls tightened, like they were looking for more to spill. I was still so turned on that I could barely catch my breath. Even more so when Ty positioned himself over me, his thick, heavy body trapping me against the bed in a way that was both threatening and the best sensation I'd ever felt.

"My omega," he purred as he kissed my shoulder and my neck, then nibbled on my earlobe. "I want my omega to be happy and satisfied. Always."

It was so primal, so trite, but I loved it. God, how I loved it! I wanted him to own me and claim me and take me however he wanted me. Because with Ty, it felt safe. It felt right. With Ty, I could let go of that ever-present need to be the one handling things, to be the responsible one, the grown-up. With Ty, I could be weak, be taken care of. I hadn't known I needed that, but God, did I ever!

With Ty's scent strong in my nose and some unseen, erotic force giving me power, I tilted my hips up against Ty and demanded, "Fuck me, alpha. Fuck me deep."

I shocked myself with the force of my demand, and I probably shocked Ty too, but he was quick to obey. He lifted up just enough for me to see the dark fire of lust in his eyes, then he worked his magic, positioning me just so, and pushed his hot, thick cock hard into me.

I let out a cry that our hosts probably heard from wherever they were in the house. And when Ty pulled back to thrust again, I let out another. It felt so good. My body felt pleasure in every cell as Ty continued to pound me, going deeper every time, but my soul sang and thrashed and danced with the pleasure of mating with my alpha.

It wasn't like heat. My womb hadn't dropped low enough for Ty's cock to reach it, no matter how long he was or how hard he pushed into me. I didn't expect things to be like they were in heat. I didn't expect them to be as bone-meltingly amazing as they turned out to be either.

I was a mess of groaning and clutching and, thank God, coming enough to fill one of the fountains in the mansion's gardens as Ty used me for his own pleasure. I'd asked him about the possibility of tamping down the bond in the bathroom, but it felt wide open and gaping like my hungry asshole as we fucked. Which made every physical sensation feel like it was limned in gold and sparkling with stardust. I knew Ty felt it too, which made it even better.

When he came deep inside me, my body responded with a coordinated orgasm to match. It was completely unexpected, but so good my eyes rolled back in my head and I ended up floating in orgasmic bliss for a bit.

When I came down from that high, I was lying in Ty's arms, still trying to catch my breath. He'd positioned us the right way around in the bed, though he hadn't pulled the covers over us, since we were both still too hot.

"That was incredible," I panted, a little too embarrassed by just how big of a slut I'd been for him to look him in the eyes.

"I'd forgotten bonding heightens everything about sex," Ty panted in return. "I've never experienced it for myself. Until now." He stroked my head and the back of my neck too, which made me burrow against him and breathe in his scent.

I think I grunted in response, but I was so fucked-out and happy that I couldn't form words. I knew it was biology, that as soon as my brain reengaged I would feel differently, but in that moment, all I cared about was being with my alpha and pleasing him.

My last thought before I fell asleep was that if all I had to worry about in life was keeping Ty sexually satisfied, I'd be golden.

Chapter Sixteen

Ty

I slept like a rock, satisfied body and soul, Winslow cradled in my arms. It was the best night of sleep I'd had in a while, and not because of the high-end mattress or sheets, although I supposed they didn't hurt.

It was all starting to come together in my mind. The leftover hormones from Winslow's heat had pretty much cleared my system, things with Sanchez and Cross had started off on an okay foot, and I was starting to see that there was a world of possibility for ways I could adjust my thinking and keep on with the career track I was passionate about.

I was so grateful that my head was in the right place again and that I could see my way through the unexpected turn in my life—a turn I was happier and happier about with each new breath Winslow took as he continued to sleep with his lips nearly pressed against my shoulder—that I slept through the alarm I'd set on my cell phone. The volume was down too low, and the phone was just out of arm's reach, so instead of hearing it and waking on time, ready for a day of business negotiations, Winslow and I were startled awake by a knock on the guestroom door.

"Mr. Martin?" a polite male voice asked from the hall. "Is everything alright? It's past nine o'clock."

It was like being awakened with a bucket of ice-cold water.

I gasped and sat straighter, knocking Winslow to the side and waking him up as I did. I stretched to grab my phone, and when I saw the time, I hissed, "Shit." I cleared my throat and called out, "Everything is fine. We just overslept is all. Sorry. Could you tell Mr. Martinez and Mrs. Cross we'll be down in a few minutes?"

"Yes, sir," the staff member said.

I heard his footsteps walk away, but only barely, as I threw back the bedcovers and hurried to the bathroom, muttering, "Shit, shit, shit, shit," under my breath the whole time.

Through the bond, I felt Winslow's rush of guilt. That made me wince as I turned on the shower and waited for the water to heat up.

"It's not your fault," I told him as he wandered into the bathroom, hugging himself and looking embarrassed to be naked in front of me. I hated that, but I didn't have time to dwell on it. "We both overslept because we were both exhausted after a tough couple of days."

I turned back to the shower, running my hand under the spray, and I could have sworn I heard Winslow say, "But if I weren't here, if we hadn't bonded...."

When I turned back to him, his mouth was firmly shut, and he stared blankly at the shower, not fully awake.

Double shit. I was hearing the edges of his thoughts now. That meant our bond was wide open and pulsing like a living thing. And yeah, that was definitely an effect of the smoking-hot sex we'd had last night, and the bond would mellow out in a few hours, but we'd probably left it wide open all through the night—which, yep, could be why I didn't hear the alarm—which would mean Winslow would be a constant presence in my head all day.

And in the mood he I knew he was in, it was going to make staying focused on negotiations for the B&M branch a huge challenge.

"I'm so sorry," Winslow said, as if he were about to burst into tears. "I've really fucked things up, haven't I."

Shit. The bond worked both ways. He'd probably just felt that thought and took the blame for it.

"Don't worry about it, baby," I said, gesturing for him to get in the shower with me. "We'll figure this out. Everything will be okay."

I forced myself to keep repeating that in my mind as I grabbed the soap and quickly scrubbed both myself and Winslow. I couldn't let my thoughts stray into dangerous territory. Winslow would feel it, and his guilt and depression would bounce back on me, making it that much harder to concentrate.

We shouldn't have had sex last night...but I didn't regret that for a second.

We showered in record time—I would have to make a point of showering with my omega again, sometime when we could truly enjoy the warm water and our soapy bodies—then jumped out, dried off, and shaved fast enough to nick my jaw a little. Winslow didn't seem like he needed to shave every day—most omegas didn't have to—but he ran a razor over his face anyhow, as if he were trying to make the best impression.

I knew he was fretting over the lack of quality in his wardrobe as we dressed, which was why I made a point of going over to him, kissing him soundly, and saying, "You look hot," before taking his hand and heading out of the room.

I crossed my fingers and hoped that being late to breakfast would be the only hiccup in the day, but life had evidently decided to be a bitch.

"You two have a nice morning fuck?" Carl asked from the pristinely set breakfast table, Sanchez at one end and Cross at the other, as Winslow and I walked into the room. Carl wore a wide, impish grin as he asked the question, but that grin vanished as he reached for his cup of coffee and ended up knocking it over and ruining the tablecloth as he did.

Mortification radiated from Winslow, causing the hair on the back of my neck to stand up as we moved to take our places at the table. Sanchez's eyes were wide with offense as he glanced from Carl to me and Winslow, and Cross gasped and tried to scoot out of the way as some of Carl's coffee threatened to drip off the table and onto her sky-blue pants suit.

"I'm so sorry," I said, focusing on damage control with Sanchez and ignoring my urge to wring Carl's neck. "I didn't hear my alarm this morning. I set the sound too low," I added, sending a quick, fierce look to Carl to let him know his little joke was not cool.

"It happens to the best of us," Sanchez said with a tight smile.

That was the only disaster that occurred during breakfast, but we ran into problems again immediately after, as all five of us crammed into one of Sanchez's sports cars—which was, thankfully, a convertible.

"Shotgun!" Carl called, racing ahead of the rest of us to where one of the staff held the door open, for Cross, I assumed.

Carl beat everyone to the car, sliding into the passenger's seat and becoming immediately absorbed in all of the car's controls.

"I'm really sorry," Winslow said, radiating humiliation that I was sure even Sanchez and Cross could feel. "We could leave my brother here, if you don't mind the possibility of him breaking something."

"Not a chance," Cross said, still smiling as the rest of us reached the car. "I like Carl's enthusiasm. He was so entertaining at breakfast, before the two of you came down. I definitely want him to meet our friend, Harrison."

I wanted Carl to meet the interior of the car's trunk, but I kept a calm smile in place and helped both Winslow and Cross into the backseat of the car while Sanchez took the wheel.

Zippy little sports cars were not designed for alphas to sit in the back seat, though. I was surprised that a car like that even had a back seat. The trip into the center of Norwalk was stiff and uncomfortable, and as usual, Carl monopolized the entire conversation.

"Does Norwalk have museums about the history of the town or about early industry in general?" he asked Sanchez—who wore a firm scowl as he concentrated on driving. "I'm really interested in the growth and development of economies of small cities like these, and I'd love to learn more."

"We do have museums," Cross answered from the back seat. "If there's time, I'll see if I can arrange a tour."

We had a little bit of a bright spot once we parked at the tall, glass building where Sanchez and Cross had the offices for their foundation. I had already started rehearsing the speeches I'd planned to sell the idea of a B&M branch, and I was mentally going through the pages of the presentation booklets in the satchel I'd fetched from my truck before heading into town, but instead of heading straight to a meeting room, Cross took us on a detour to an office on the ground floor.

"This is the headquarters for our housing development project," she explained as we stepped inside. "And this is

Harrison Rice, the project manager for our Walker Drive neighborhood."

Cross introduced all of us to Rice, but as nice as the man seemed to be—I could tell he was a beta, though he was tall and broad, like an alpha, with a salt of the earth, no nonsense attitude—and as fascinating as the work he did was, I was anxious to get started with the B&M negotiations.

It wasn't until Cross said, "Harrison, I thought you might let Carl here tag along with you to the project today. Glen won't mind. We talked about it this morning, and Carl would love to learn more about what we're doing to build affordable housing, and maybe help out for the day while his brother and Mr. Martin discuss the possible Bangers & Mash branch with us."

It hit me in a rush what Cross was doing and how brilliant she was. I could feel that Winslow was taken by surprise by her ninja-like move as well.

"I'd love to see what you guys are doing." Carl lit up like someone had just handed him a sparkler at a supper picnic. "I'm really handy with a hammer too."

"Excellent," Harrison said. "We're just about to load up the truck, if you want to help with that too. I can introduce you to the site foreman, Glen Bolden."

"Sure," Carl said with a smile.

And just like that, with a knowing nod to me and a smile for Winslow, Rice thumped Carl's back and led him off to what I assumed was a back entrance and work that needed to be done.

Cross turned to me and Winslow with what my papa would have called a "shit-eating grin". "I called Harrison last night, after supper," she said. "I figured everyone would be happier if he had something constructive to focus on, no pun intended."

My admiration for the woman grew a thousandfold. She

was the perfect partner for Bangers & Mash. I could already see all the ways she would work tirelessly for the benefit of omegas, and she probably had it in her to charm Norwalk's city council into enthusiastic agreement with whatever plans they came up with that day too.

"Thank you," I said, sending her a significant look. I rested my hand on the small of Winslow's back and added, "I am constantly amazed at the things omegas can get done when they're encouraged to spread their wings."

"Yes, we are a crafty lot," Cross said, winking at Winslow.

We walked out of the office and headed up to a third-floor conference room, and I was absolutely certain the day would be nothing but smooth sailing and calm seas from there on out.

I wish I'd been right.

The committee from Norwalk's city council was already pacing the conference room by the time we got there. I noticed right away that every one of them to a man—and they were all men—was an alpha, and they were dressed in suits. Somehow, even in her sky-blue pants suit, with the force of her personality alone, Cross fit in.

Winslow stuck out like a sore thumb in blue jeans.

Worse still, he knew it. I felt his awkward embarrassment like a knife in my heart.

"Mr. Martin, it's a pleasure to meet you at last," a man I recognized as Roger Crane, the head of the planning committee from the city that I'd spoken with on video chat a few times, stepped forward and held out his hand to me. I took his hand, but before I could say anything, Crane sniffed slightly and smiled at Winslow a bit too openly and asked, "And who have we here?"

I forced myself to fight off the roar of alpha possessiveness that slammed into me at Crane's too-sharp interest in my omega. "This is my omega, Winslow Grant," I said, unable to stop myself from sliding an arm around Winslow's waist and pulling him close...claiming him.

"Lucky you," Crane said, laughing, his eyes bright with lust.

I could practically feel a growl rising up in me. It took everything I had to tamp it down. I needed to play nice with the Norwalk city council if we had a hope of banging out the B&M branch deal. But men like Crane—who didn't seem to recognize boundaries and who probably thought all omegas were fair game for whichever alpha wanted them—were exactly the reason why B&M was necessary in the first place.

"Let's get started, why don't we," Sanchez said, watching the interaction with a disapproving expression.

I wished I knew whether he disapproved of Crane's behavior or of Winslow's presence. Maybe it was both.

For his part, Winslow did an amazing job of holding his own—though he did it without speaking—as we all took seats around the conference table for the initial presentation. He even handed out the booklets for me, though I noticed he kept as far away from Crane, and some of the other alphas, as he could. I could feel how relieved he was to sit beside me and blend into the furniture as I launched into an explanation of the costs and benefits of a B&M branch.

Again, my hopes that everything would go smoothly from there were dashed.

I had a hard time paying attention to my own presentation, and I stammered and lost my place more than once. The Norwalk councilmen probably thought it was some sort of incompetence on my part—which I hated with the flames of a thousand suns—but it was actually the constant pulse of anxiety and barely controlled panic from Winslow that made the numbers and tables on the charts I was working from dance around, like toddlers streaking naked through a yard full of puppies, all of them hopped up on sugar.

The fact that my mind went straight to toddlers and puppies, and my imagination filled in a laughing, round-bellied Winslow chasing after them, everyone joyful and content, was a whole other layer of distraction I really didn't need with a project this big on the line.

The trouble was, the more I talked, the more I was aware that Crane and one or two of the others were watching Winslow. The more they did, the more uncomfortable Winslow felt, which meant the more uncomfortable I felt. Which muddled my presentation even more.

I was deeply grateful when I reached the end of it to have Sanchez speak up with, "Why don't we visit the site my wife has picked out to potentially be the Bangers & Mash office. It's just a short walk from here."

"I would love to see what you have in mind," I said with a nod of gratitude for Sanchez.

However stoic the man was, and however much he disapproved of Carl, Sanchez was on my side—my and Winslow's side. He and Cross subtly put themselves between me and Winslow and Crane as we headed out of the office, me answering simple questions about B&M operations and profit margins, until we got outside and started down the tree-lined street.

"To be honest," Crane said, deliberately positioning himself to walk next to me and Winslow, despite Sanchez and Cross's efforts, "I'm not sold on the idea of such an impersonal and cold method of taking omegas through heat." He looked a little too keenly at Winslow as he spoke. "I'm more of a traditionalist. Whatever happened to the days when omegas were focused on settling down with a solid and dependable mate and preserving their heat for their alpha?"

The question twisted my stomach with loathing, mostly because I'd heard those sentiments enough to know they were code for keeping omegas out of public life and confining them to traditional roles, whether that was what they wanted from their lives or not.

"The philosophy behind emergency heat support, and the reason why Bangers & Mash was founded, was to give omegas the freedom to pursue their own lives on their own time, to have careers and to follow their dreams and ambitions instead of being given only one choice—to be a homemaker."

"What do you have against homemakers?" Crane demanded.

"Nothing at all," I said, trying to think fast while feeling Winslow's extreme discomfort. "If that's what an omega wants to do."

"And what do you want from your life, young Winslow?" Crane glanced past me to grin hungrily at my omega. "Do you want to waffle about in the big, bad world, or would you rather stay safe at home, protected by your alpha, raising his children?"

Crane had no idea how low of a blow his question was, considering the things Winslow and I had talked about where the course of his life was concerned.

"I...I don't really know," Winslow answered meekly.

"You see?" Crane argued. "It's so much easier for an omega when they have an alpha to guide them. This nonsense of impersonal heat servicing feels more like prostitution to me than anything else."

"Here we are," Cross announced, her voice high and sharp, as we reached a small building that looked as though it had just been built. It stood at the edge of a development where half a dozen houses were under construction, with lots for at least two dozen more. "We're proposing that the Bangers & Mash office be located here, within our Walker Drive neighborhood."

I could tell from her stiff, almost combative posture that

she hated Crane's line of logic as much as I did, and that she'd had to deal with it for a while.

"We figure at least one of the other houses could serve as facilities for ESA calls, particularly for omegas on a budget who might not be able to afford the additional cost of a hotel room," Sanchez said, quietly taking his wife's hand and stepping up to defend her, and all the omegas of Norwalk. He rose in my estimation as he did.

Crane snorted and muttered, "Hotel rooms," under his breath. "You know who else uses hotel rooms that way?"

I moved closer to Winslow, scrambling to manage his panic enough to help me think clearly. Crane wasn't the only councilman who seemed to feel that way about the project, but not all of the councilmen shared his opinion. In fact, as Sanchez and Cross took us through the newly constructed house, I got the idea that most of them were probably in favor of the idea, but that they were beholden to Crane somehow.

If I could just concentrate long enough to present the B&M plan to those councilmen, I was sure I could convince them to sign on the dotted line for the branch. I needed to do something, because it was becoming apparent that the deal wasn't as done as I'd thought it was.

If I'd known about Crane's opinions, if I'd known there was more work to do, I might have tried to figure out a way to leave Winslow at home. I might have sent someone else in my place. It was just too hard to think with the newness of the bond and the intensity of the emotions I was borrowing from Winslow.

We'd gone through the house and reached a point where Cross stopped to explain something to Crane and the councilmen, and were standing near a large, bay window that looked out over the rest of the street when Winslow inched up to me.

"Hey, I think I see Carl out there, working," he said in a

soft, defeated voice. "Would you mind if I joined him instead of sticking around the meetings?"

His question meant way more than that. I didn't need a bond to sense it. He was uncomfortable and out of place with the likes of Crane, and he knew he was interfering with my ability to do my job. It wasn't lost on me that, once again, being bonded had thrown a wrench in my career plans.

A large part of me didn't want to let him go, but sense won out. "Are you sure you'll be okay?" I asked, brushing my fingers over his cheek.

Winslow nodded, looking up at me with sad, regret-filled eyes. "I'll be fine."

I didn't believe him. Something was wrong. It felt like we were back where we'd started—him beating himself up because he believed he'd wrecked my life and me wanting to help him, but not knowing how. And I had other responsibilities on top of that.

I didn't care who was watching, I cupped his face and tilted it up to kiss his lips. "If you start to get a headache or feel sick because of the bond, come back to me, okay?" I said as my way of letting him go.

Winslow smiled, but wouldn't quite meet my eyes. "I... sure," he said.

That answer was anything but reassuring.

"Okay, baby," I whispered, then kissed him again. "Stay safe."

I felt relief swell up through the bond, but it hurt a little to feel that as Winslow walked away, like he was relieved to be rid of me. There wasn't any logic in that thought, but I felt it anyhow.

And honestly, as I felt the bond stretch and my thoughts clear, we both probably needed a bit of time alone. Bonds and relationships were always a balancing act, and since mine and

Winslow's was so new, we hadn't had time to figure out how to make ours work best.

"So, Mr. Crane, let me answer your question about why emergency heat support is so necessary," I said, stepping back into the fray and feeling far more confident as I did.

I could do this. I could convince an ass like Crane to free up the money for Norwalk to open a B&M branch. I could do it for Winslow, because omegas like Winslow needed what B&M did. And because I needed Winslow.

Chapter Seventeen

Winslow

I was definitely ruining Ty's life. Knowing that in my head was one thing, but seeing it in action as Ty stumbled through his presentation when he needed to nail it was another. Worse still, I knew a lot of Ty's missteps were because that gross Mr. Crane kept looking at me like he wished he'd been the one to find me in the hotel vestibule last week.

Ty could feel my anxiety about the man, which angered him, which worried me, which worried him...and it was all just a gigantic clusterfuck. How did bonded mates even function in the world anyhow?

I knew the answer to that too. Most bonded mates had been together forever. They weren't stupidly mismatched either. Like Mr. Sanchez and Mrs. Cross. I could tell they were bonded—it was like I knew what to look for now to see things like that—but they were both rich and sophisticated and fit together.

Ty and I fit together like a peanut butter and onion sandwich.

I had to do something about it. And no, it wasn't just heat hormones or the shock of a new life. I *had* to make this whole thing better.

The irony of me showing up to bother Carl when he was in the middle of working wasn't lost on me as I searched for him at the construction sites. There were a lot of men—and a few women—working on two or three of the houses that were in various stages of construction in the little neighborhood. I liked the entire concept of the neighborhood. It impressed me that someone would be so kind as to construct low-cost houses for people who really needed them, like me and Carl. I wondered what things would have been like if we'd had someplace like this to live instead of Mr. Caruthers's grubby apartment.

Carl was actually hard at work on one of the crews that was erecting premade wall frames. I hung back for a second and watched. A crane of some sort had lifted the wall piece and was maneuvering it into position. Carl—wearing a hardhat, goggles, and gloves—was part of the crew that helped guide the piece into place, then held it while a bunch of other men did whatever they were doing—I couldn't see from where I stood—to secure the frame to the foundation, and to nail it into the other wall, which had already been set in place.

Despite everything, I smiled as I watched Carl work. He nodded to a guy who I guessed was a foreman and jumped to follow whatever instructions he'd been given that I hadn't heard clearly. Thank God they hadn't given him one of the nail guns, but that didn't seem to bother Carl.

I leaned against the side of the house where I'd stopped to watch, crossed my arms, and frowned in thought. Carl was a good worker when he had someone to keep him focused on his task, like he did just then. I didn't want to disturb him, so I stood there and watched for a long time as the crew finished up with the one wall, then brought in another. The process was fascinating, and I found myself actually proud of Carl as he blended right in with the rest of the workers.

The ghost of the idea that Carl might not actually need me after all, that he could stand on his own two feet, as long as he had the right ground under him, felt weird. It had only ever been me and him and Mom, and now it was just me and him. I didn't know if letting Carl go would be the end of things for the two of us, or if it would strengthen our relationship, because it wouldn't be so codependent anymore.

And if Carl could be on his own, what did that mean for me and Ty?

Gingerly, not wanting to disturb Ty while he was busy doing things that were way more important than me, I closed my eyes and concentrated on our bond. It was way more peaceful now. It sort of hummed instead of...I don't know, spiking, like it had been doing before. I could feel Ty's confidence, feel his focus, though it was in the distance. There was no frustration and very little worry. He was getting the job done.

He didn't need me. He was only able to do what he was best at if I wasn't there.

That thought would have depressed me to the point of sinking to sit in the pile of dirt around the edge of the new house I leaned against if Carl hadn't walked up to me, wiping his forehead with the back of his sleeve as he did.

"What are you doing here?" he asked breathlessly. He'd picked up a bottle of water somewhere and unscrewed the cap to take a long drink. "I thought you were doing important Bangers & Mash stuff."

I shrugged, glancing down at my scuffed shoes as I kicked

the dirt. "Ty doesn't really need me up there," I said. Ty didn't really need me at all. "It's just a bunch of guys in suits, most of them alphas. I don't really fit in, and I'm just distracting him."

Carl shrugged in confusion and scrunched up his face for a second. "How are you distracting him? He likes having you around. He really likes you, Winslow."

I glanced up and met Carl's eyes with a flat look. "He only likes me because we accidentally bonded during my heat."

God. I hadn't even thought of that until the words were out of my mouth. No wonder Ty was so distracted. He was probably inundated with all the fake feels that only happened because of some pretty intense biology.

Although that didn't explain last night, a part of my mind whispered. Last night had been something else.

"Oh, he likes you alright," Carl said after taking another long drink. "Everyone can tell that. And I was looking up stuff about bonding on Ty's computer the other night. Bonds only ever happen between people who like each other a lot."

"I barely knew Ty when it happened," I argued, brow dropped into a frown.

"Yeah, but you liked him," Carl pointed out.

"How do you know? You weren't even there." I didn't know why I was being so belligerent and immature. That was usually Carl's job. But there he was, looking all purposeful and grown up. When did our roles reverse?

"I'm just guessing," Carl said, "because I've known you your whole life. But my guess is that you liked him because he rescued you. He was nice to you. You guys had super-hot sex, but knowing what I know about Ty now, and about you, you probably talked a whole lot between heat waves, and he probably went out of his way to make you feel comfortable, because as far as I've seen, that's just who Ty is."

I blinked and uncrossed my arms. Carl was right...which was so weird to begin with.

"Okay," I sighed. "You're right. I did like him right from the start." And not just because he was pounding my heat-soaked womb with that magic cock of his and making me lose my mind with pleasure. "But that doesn't change the fact that he's way out of my league and that I'm a massive liability to him."

Carl laughed, then finished the last of his water. "You? Winslow Grant? A liability? Have you been paying attention to yourself for the last five years or so?"

"What's that supposed to mean?" I asked, rolling my shoulders. I wasn't sure I knew how to deal with Carl when he was making sense.

Carl smacked his lips and sighed as he finished his water, then gestured for me to follow him over to a recycling bin on the other side of the street. "You're always taking care of people," he said as we walked. "You took care of Mom, you take care of me—even though I don't need it, mind you."

"Um, yeah, you do," I said, tempted to cross my arms again.

"Whatever," Carl said, tossing his empty bottle at the recycling bin and missing. He turned to me and said, "The point is, you're not some sort of liability to Ty, the way I'm a liability to you."

I didn't expect those words to hit me square in the chest the way they did. "You're not a liability to me, Carl," I insisted.

Carl laughed. "How many dates have you been on since Mom died? How many things have you given up to save my sorry ass from having too much fun?"

I quirked one eyebrow up. "Having fun?"

"I'm just trying to live my life, and you keep getting in the way," he said with a smile, spreading his arms to the side, like he'd won the point. I could tell he was just messing with me, though.

I crossed my arms again. "Pick up that bottle and put it in the bin where it belongs," I said.

"See?" Carl said, bending to fetch the bottle and toss it in the bin. "And I know I haven't exactly been easy," he started to go on.

"Carl!" the man I'd assumed was the foreman of the building project called from the house they were working on. "We're ready to do the fourth wall."

"Okay, Glen! I'll be right there," Carl called back. He faced me again with a bright smile. "Who would have thought that construction work would be so cool? I mean, they're probably breaking all sorts of laws by letting me help out, since I don't know what the fuck I'm doing, but it's not really that hard to hold something in place while other guys nail it."

He paused and tilted his head to the side, then said, "I'm sure there's a sex joke in there, but that's really your thing now, isn't it."

He was teasing. I scowled at him.

Carl laughed again and went on. "I'm hoping they'll let me use the nail gun later on. Those things are cool as fuck. But Glen said I really would have to undergo some training before they'd let me do that."

"Carl!" Glen called out again.

"Coming!" Carl called back, rocking forward.

He paused to thump my arm. "Stop sweating the small stuff, Winslow. You're not a distraction, and Ty really does like you."

"But the bond," I argued. "It's not a good thing for Ty. It's messed up his whole life."

Carl still didn't seem to see the point I was making. He shrugged once again as he headed across the street to the construction site. "So? Build a new one. Or maybe I could help you," he added, his smile broadening, "since I'm an expert in building things now."

I smiled in return, but honestly, I didn't know how to feel as my brother jogged back to join the construction crew. The thought that Carl didn't need me anymore was too big for me to swallow. Granted, it had only been a few hours, and knowing Carl, he'd get tired of what he was doing before the end of the day, then he'd be back in my hair...just like I would be back in Ty's if I returned to the office building and interrupted his meeting.

It was a shitty position to be in—like I was some sort of trapeze artist who had let go of one swing and was reaching for the next, but with no idea if I would be able to complete the trick or if I would plunge to my death on the floor of the circus below.

I forced myself to shake away from that thought—particularly because I felt a whisper of concern from the bond, like Ty had caught that thought and wasn't happy about it. I doubted he had actually heard or felt my thoughts. We were too far apart—I could tell because of the slight headache nagging me—and even if we weren't, I still didn't want him to get distracted by me when he was doing something important.

Which was really what it all boiled down to. I couldn't keep messing things up for people. I didn't want to be a burden to Ty. I didn't want to distract Carl from something he might actually be good at doing and that he liked, even if it was just one day of helping out. If Carl decided he enjoyed construction work, maybe he could find a job doing it when we returned to Barrington. I didn't want to get in the way of his life either.

With a huff of determination, I thrust my hands into my jeans pockets and walked back up the street to the office building. But once I got there, I turned right and headed along the main road and away from the office building again. A walk was what I needed. I needed to stretch my legs, get as far away from the people whose lives I was bringing down with my presence as possible, and maybe look for something to do that would catch my interest, the way construction might have captured Carl's. Ty was stuck with me now, but that didn't mean I had to be completely useless.

The section of Norwalk where the new neighborhood and the office building were located was an okay area, but not the center of town, or as upper-class an area as I would have expected people like Mr. Sanchez and Mrs. Cross to work in. There were plenty of small shops for me to look into and a few cafés and diners that made my stomach growl, since it was more or less lunchtime. I didn't know what I was looking for as I explored the area, but I hoped something would jump out at me, something that would tell me what I wanted to do with the rest of my life. Maybe even something that would tell me how to fix the mess I'd made of Ty's life.

It was kind of ironic that, just as I was pondering how to fix the life of an alpha that I'd accidentally bonded with, I walked past a slightly run-down omega services clinic. The place looked like every other community outreach center I'd ever come across, with worn linoleum floors, plastic chairs lining the room, a shabby desk where a tired, middle-aged beta sat, and posters on the walls that informed about childcare options, birth control, and low-level job training.

Something about the place was as depressing as it was encouraging, but I grabbed the door handle, swung it open, and walked inside anyhow. The place had a gently clinical smell to it—sweet, like omegas, which I didn't usually pick up, so it must have been strong. I wondered how they kept predatory alphas away. Two omegas sat on some of the plastic chairs on the side of the room, a young man and a young woman, both with fussy babies in their arms. They seemed happy enough to be waiting for whatever they were waiting for, but they stopped their conversation to glance up at me when I came in.

THE WRONG OMEGA

"Can I help you?" the beta behind the desk said.

He had a kind smile, so I approached.

Before I could think about it or stop myself, I asked, "What do you know about bonding?"

"Bonding?" he asked, blinking.

"Yeah. Like, is it possible to break a bond if you think it was a mistake?" I felt icy shivers pour down my back and my headache throb harder at the base of my skull as the question escaped from me. "It's not for me," I added in a rush, lying through my teeth. "It's for a friend of mine. He thinks the bond with his alpha was a mistake, and he wants to get out of it. But is that even possible?"

The beta looked up at me with eyes that said he knew damn well I was talking about myself. There was a hint of compassion in those eyes as well.

"Bonds don't form by accident," he said, getting up and moving to a wall full of informational brochures. "They usually take a lifetime to form at all. Although I have heard of some cases of heat-induced bonding that happens suddenly."

It was like someone had flicked on the light. "Yeah, I'm sure that's what it was. Is there a way to break a bond like that? Especially...especially if it kind of ruins the alpha's life?"

The beta's brows shot all the way up at my question. He'd pulled a couple of pamphlets from the display and handed them to me, but he also lowered his voice to ask, "Have you talked to your alpha about this, honey? He might not feel the same way."

"It's not for me, it's for a friend," I insisted, my face going hot with the lie as I snatched the pamphlets from him. One was about post-heat syndrome, and the other was about bonding. "But thanks for your help."

I turned and marched out of the clinic, pissed off at myself for going in to begin with. I didn't need complete strangers second-guessing my feelings without knowing the first thing about me. The facts were the facts. I'd ended Ty's life as he knew it, and neither of us knew what it would look like now, or if the damage I'd been done could be fixed.

As I reached the street corner, my headache growing slightly in intensity, and was about to throw the pamphlets in a trashcan, a whisper of, "Hey," caught my attention.

I turned back to find the male omega who had been in the clinic hurrying after me, his baby against his shoulder. A thread of panic hit me, but he was only another omega, and a father at that. So I waited until he caught up.

"I heard what you were asking about in there," he said in a low voice when he reached me.

"I was asking for a friend," I said, lying again.

The omega shook his head like he didn't care. "Are you bonded to an asshole or something?" he asked. I opened my mouth, riddled with guilt, no clue how I should reply—because Ty definitely wasn't an asshole—but the omega rushed on. "Listen, it happens to the best of us. We end up stuck with the wrong alpha. They're possessive, abusive, and mean. I can imagine it would be even worse if you were bonded to one."

I could suddenly see the poor guy's entire story, even though he wasn't overtly talking about himself. He was that omega who'd been stuck with a rotten alpha. And he'd had a baby with the guy too. And if he was seeking out omega services, the jerk had probably left him with a baby and very little money or hope.

Which was exactly the sort of situation Ty said Bangers & Mash existed to prevent.

I felt an unexpected rush of longing for Ty to be successful with his meeting and his desire to help omegas.

With it, my headache pounded, and my back began to spasm.

"There is a way to break a bond," the omega said, snapping me out of those thoughts so quickly I jerked. The omega looked this way and that, like he was going to try to sell me drugs or something. "I heard this from a reliable source, but apparently, you can break a bond by having sex with someone else, another alpha. That snaps pretty much any bond quickly. But they don't want us to know that. They want to keep us on their leashes, like good little bitches."

"I...um...yeah, I guess that makes sense," I said, feeling sorrier for the omega than ever. God, his life must be terrible. Way worse than mine. Norwalk definitely needed more support for omegas, in their culture as well as institutionally.

It did make sense that having sex with another alpha could break a bond. It was a kind of betrayal, after all, which would break any relationship.

Maybe bonds were actually formed and broken way more frequently than people let on. Maybe the only reason people thought bonds only happened with long-term couples was because the ones that formed between people who barely knew each other were broken so quickly.

Maybe I could set Ty free after all.

"I just wanted to let you know," the omega said, bouncing his baby in his arms as it started to fuss. "Do with that information what you will."

"Okay, thanks," I said as he turned to walk back to the clinic.

My gaze instantly traveled past him, way down to the end of the street, to a small group of men in suits. Not just any men either. I recognized them as some of the city councilors from the meeting. They must have broken for lunch.

More than that, I recognized creepy Mr. Crane with them.

Just about the time Mr. Crane looked up and spotted me.

A toothy grin split Mr. Crane's face, and he waved to me.

He said something to the other two councilors, then picked up his pace as he walked toward me.

Suddenly, I had a really clear idea of how I could break my bond with Ty and un-ruin his life.

Chapter Eighteen

Ty

It was frustrating. With my head back on my shoulders, I breezed through my prepared presentation and answered every question the Norwalk city councilmen had without batting an eyelash. My confidence had never been higher, and my passion for what I did shone through with everything I said. I was clear-headed, demonstrated competence, and within an hour, with Sanchez and Cross glowing like I'd done them a personal favor, I'd convinced the councilmen to go all in with the B&M branch.

It was one of the shining moments of my career, but it felt hollow and aggravating, because I'd had to push Winslow away in order to have it.

Winslow had been right all along. Being bonded was a distraction. Having my omega there by my side had drawn my focus and muddled my thinking. I'd only been able to do my job without him there.

"That was fantastic," Cross said as she and Sanchez came over to congratulate me once we'd broken for lunch. "You had them eating out of your hands. I knew bringing you in to make the presentation would be what won the city council over."

"You don't look happy about it," Sanchez said with a concerned frown.

I took a split second to decide whether to brush over the whole thing or whether to be honest as the three of us wandered out into the hallway. Several of the councilmen, including that waste of space, Crane, stood at the opposite end of the hall, chatting. I glanced to them briefly, caught Crane's eye, nodded, then turned back to Cross and Sanchez.

"I'm very happy about what we've done and what we will continue to do for Norwalk," I said. "I think a Bangers & Mash branch will do a lot of good here."

"But?" Sanchez pressed me.

If the man hadn't had a way of looking deadly serious about everything, I might have made up an excuse. But the probing way he had of looking at people—I'd seen him do it with the councilors in the meeting too—made me want to confess everything. He would have made a great high school principal in another life.

I blew out a breath and rubbed a hand over the bottom half of my face. "I feel awful for sending Winslow away like that."

Cross blinked in surprise. "You didn't send him away. I thought he decided to stretch his legs and go find his brother." Which was what I'd told them when they asked about it during the earlier break.

"He did," I went on with a wince, "but I feel like I chased him off. Worse still, it was so much easier for me to concentrate without him sitting next to me, with the bond turned down a little. Though at the same time, I keep feeling like something's missing. But I do a better job of things when that is missing, and I can't help but feel—"

I stopped there. I really was skating into some seriously unprofessional territory now, and I needed to put a lid on it. Lack of concentration wasn't the only way to tank a meeting, or a career. Talking about my omega to the people I was meant to be working with like I was a lovesick schoolboy was not a good look for someone about to be entrusted with a multi-million-dollar expansion project.

To my surprise, it was Sanchez who smiled forgivingly. "Didn't you say your bond was brand new?"

I wasn't certain how much I wanted to confide in the couple. "Yeah. Less than a week old."

Sanchez and Cross exchanged a knowing smile.

Cross laughed as she turned to me and said, "Yeah, that explains it. It took us a while to learn how to manage being bonded too. The good news is that it's not always like trying to run a three-legged race with your partner."

"The concentration thing gets much easier over time," Sanchez added thumping my arm. "You'll be fine in a couple of weeks."

I was encouraged by that statement, but it didn't help me deal with the nerves and emotions that were messing with me right then and there, when I had a major business plan to execute and a deal to seal.

"We're treating everyone to lunch at the Riverwalk Café," Cross went on. "It's just up the street a little. You'll join us, of course."

"Of course," I answered, forcing myself to smile. "I just need to call the office to let them know how the meeting went, and then find Winslow."

It didn't feel right for me to put those two things in that order.

"We'll save you a seat," Sanchez said, then took his wife's hand and headed to the elevators.

It was the first overt sign of affection I'd seen between the pair. I noted it because the gesture didn't make them look any less professional than I knew them to be.

Which meant that maybe there was hope for me and Winslow after all. Winslow wasn't as polished or sophisticated as Madeline Cross, but he didn't have to be, and honestly, I wouldn't have wanted him to be.

I liked Winslow's laid-back, casual feeling of youth. I liked the wide-eyed way he looked at the world, like everything was new. He wasn't jaded yet. He was just tired, after everything he'd had to endure for the last few years. I loved how strong he was for making it through everything, and I loved the vastness of the potential he had.

I loved him. It was as simple as that. I didn't need months and months to get to know him. Getting to know someone on that level happened pretty quick when you took them through heat and were wide open with them from the start. And so what if the love had happened first and all the confirmation that I was right to fall hard for the scrappy young omega came afterwards? I loved him, and that was all that mattered.

I turned toward the elevator, deciding to look for Winslow first and then to call Sal to tell him how the meeting went. I had just started to open myself up to the bond a little more as a tool to figure out where Winslow had gone when Crane walked up behind me.

"Good job in there, Mr. Martin," Crane said, his tone sounding anything but pleased. "You really knocked it out of the park." His sarcasm thickened.

Instantly, I closed up the bond—I wasn't even sure how I knew how to do it—as a way to protect Winslow from Crane's edgy, borderline vicious smile.

"I'm glad the council sees things our way and wants to

proceed with the project," I said, not sure what Crane wanted from me.

Crane plunked a hand on my shoulder, like we were two alphas on the same football team, and steered me toward the elevator.

"You and I know the way things really work," he said in a voice that had the hair standing up on the back of my head. "We know the way the world should be."

I frowned, deeply on my guard. "I'm not sure what you mean."

The elevator dinged, and the two of us got in. A pair of Crane's colleagues got in with us, but they were deep in their own discussion.

"All these measures to make life *easier* for omegas?" he went on, saying the word "easier" as though it were a joke. "They just fill omega heads with nonsense about getting above themselves."

"I beg your pardon?" I was deeply grateful when the elevator opened so I could get out and put some distance between me and Crane.

Crane chuckled. "I've done a lot of research about Bangers & Mash," he went on, walking with me to the door. "I've seen the alpha turnover rate. It's a clever game you've got going on there, Martin."

"I'm not sure I understand your meaning," I said, though actually, I was beginning to think I did, and I didn't like it.

We stopped just outside the building, and the other two councilmen walked on, but paused to wait for us at the curb.

"Bangers & Mash is a brilliant way to nudge uppity omegas who think they're mini-alphas in disguise to get married and start families, like they're supposed to," Crane said. "That's why you people go through so many alphas. They're always bonding with those uptight omegas and leaving your company to take care of them, as nature intended.

Even you did it," he added just as I opened my mouth to protest.

"Bangers & Mash is not a dating service," I said. "And me bonding with Winslow was incidental and extraordinarily rare." That wasn't entirely accurate, but I was hesitant to say much else. I knew Crane, or alphas like him. I knew that those sorts of opinions couldn't be changed with a few quick words. They could only be changed with action and by allowing omegas to thrive and prove him wrong.

Crane chuckled as if I'd agreed with him. "Well," he said, thumping my arm again, "if you decide you don't want that tasty little omega of yours after all, I'd happily take him off your hands."

I was shocked and enraged, but Crane just winked, then peeled off to join his councilmen friends. They headed up the street toward what looked like a row of small shops and businesses.

Part of me wanted to march after Crane and set him straight—and to tell him that Winslow was not some shiny bauble that I would ever dream of trading around, especially not with the likes of him. But again, men like that wouldn't have their opinions changed with one conversation.

Instead, I turned toward the construction sites lining the street that ran perpendicular to the street with the café and started my search for Winslow. Anger made it hard for me to focus on the bond as a way of finding him—it kept trying to tell me Winslow had gone up the street, the same direction Crane had just gone in, when I knew for a fact he'd headed off in search of Carl. On top of that, my phone rang in my pocket just as I stepped past the first newly constructed house.

I only picked up the call because Sal's name flashed on the screen.

"Hey, boss," I said as I searched around the half-constructed houses for my omega. "I was just about to call you."

"Good," Sal said. "How is the meeting going?"

"Very good," I said, though my tone didn't reflect my enthusiasm. "Norwalk has greenlighted the branch. We're going to discuss details about where to start and how to proceed with the whole thing."

I was so busy looking around for Winslow with an increasing sense of wrongness and dread that I almost didn't hear Sal say, "Fantastic. I knew you'd come through for us. Which is why we want you to head up that office."

I stopped where I was, between a house with workers busy hammering away and another group that looked like they'd just broken for lunch.

"Me?" I asked, blinking.

Sal laughed on the other end of the call. "Yes, Ty, you. Of course, you. After all the work you've put into this branch over the last few months, why would it be anyone but you?"

"Uh, because I can't be an ESA anymore?" I told him, frustrated that he wasn't seeing things as they were. "We'd discussed that, with the budget we'll be starting out with, it'll be all hands on deck with this office. I know this was supposed to be my gig, but you need someone who can be an ESA to coordinate the project or else it will be a waste of salary."

Sal chuckled on the other end of the line. "You really don't realize how important you are to this company and how much we value your knowledge and experience, do you."

It was a glowing compliment, but something about it hit me off-center. Hadn't I just been thinking the same thing about Winslow? That he didn't realize how strong and how competent he was, or how much potential he had? I was willing to do whatever it took to work with him instead of just making do, and now it seemed like Sal was saying the same thing about me and my relationship to B&M.

Maybe Winslow and I were a hell of a lot more alike than we'd ever stopped to consider. Bonds didn't form by accident, after all. Wasn't that what everyone had said all along?

Now I knew what that really meant, what it really felt like.

"I don't think it will be too big of a hurdle to move you to Norwalk to head up that office," Sal went on. "I just think the first thing we need to do is open the ESA training program so that we can staff up as quickly as possible. You've taught the course before. You're licensed to teach and certify other ESAs."

"But the money," I said, starting to allow myself to feel hopeful.

"We'll find it," Sal said. I could hear him shrug as well. "I'm sure there will be donors aplenty once you do a little PR about the value of emergency heat support. And hey, maybe your clever omega could take part in that. He seems like the sort who might like advocacy work, once he has a little training in it himself."

I all but caught my breath at the suggestion. Winslow probably would like advocating for omegas. He might enjoy working alongside me too. Maybe that could stop him from thinking that he was working against me just by existing, and from believing he'd ruined my life. Hell, plenty of alpha and omega pairs ended up working together. Sal and Nick were a perfect example. So were Sanchez and Cross. In fact, if we moved to Norwalk, I wouldn't mind having Cross mentor Winslow at all.

"You know that phrase, 'this might just be crazy enough to work'?" I told Sal with a growing smile.

Sal laughed. "I knew you'd like the idea. Okay, I don't want to keep you from your job for long," he continued. "Get in there and seal the deal."

"Will do," I said, then ended the call.

Hope filled me more than it had all week. I didn't know

why I hadn't seen how this could all fit together before. I wasn't seeing the forest through the trees, which was probably part hormones from Winslow's heat and part me being a stubborn ass who was certain he knew exactly how his life would play out in every detail. Things changed all the time, though, and I could easily change and adapt with them. Winslow and I could change and adapt forever.

I wanted him to be right there with me, right in that second, so I could tell him the good news and talk to him about his part in it. But even when I opened myself to our bond, he felt far away. Which didn't make any sense, because he'd said he was going to find Carl. Except, even as I thought that, I spotted Carl working along with the crew who was finishing up something in one of the construction sites, and Winslow was nowhere in sight.

Carl noticed me watching and called to a tall, burly man in a hardhat, then carefully made his way out of the frame of a house and over to me.

"Where's Winslow?" he asked as soon as he reached me.

It was pretty much exactly the opposite of what I'd hoped he would say.

"I thought he'd come out here to see you," I said, frowning as a heightened sense of anxiety started to creep in on me.

"He was," Carl said, itching the back of his head under his hardhat. "We talked a little. I told him I was having fun working on the site here, but how I wished they'd let me try the nail gun. They won't, by the way," he rushed on before I could even think of making a comment. "But Glen says he'd be willing to hire me for his crew and train me, if I was really serious about wanting to help out. And I am, weirdly enough. There's just something about being able to move all day, and not while stuck in a store, working retail, that works for me. It doesn't hurt that Glen is hot. Debbie's not half bad either." He ended with a broad smile.

I didn't even know where to start with everything he'd just spewed out. Glen and Debbie? Carl with a nail gun?

I blinked. Carl had been offered a job? In Norwalk? I would have to find out if this Glen person was serious. If he was...well, it was perfect. So perfect I wondered if, once again, Cross had grasped the situation quickly the day before, then pulled some strings today as a way of tying me to Norwalk and convincing me to really fight for the B&M location.

That woman was a dynamo, and I definitely wanted Winslow to learn everything she could teach him.

Which brought me back around to the reason I was there.

"When did Winslow leave and which direction did he head in?" I asked.

Carl shrugged. "It was at least half an hour ago, probably more. He said he needed a walk to clear his head and think about some things." Carl's face pinched with guilt. "He still thinks he ruined your life, you know."

"I know," I sighed. "And he didn't. Maybe exactly the opposite of that. I just got some news he might like to hear. The branch has been greenlighted, and Sal wants me to head it up. He wants to figure out how to integrate Winslow into things too."

Carl lit up like the morning sky. "We're moving to Norwalk?" he asked. "You mean, I really can tell Glen I'll come work for him?"

My mouth dropped open, and my first instinct was to contradict Carl and tell him Winslow and I needed our own space. Which was true, but just because Carl moved to Norwalk with us didn't mean he had to live with us. In fact, I was certain Winslow would be happy to separate from his brother a little without having to break their bond entirely.

Thinking about bonds had me catching my breath. Mine

with Winslow suddenly felt stretched too thin, almost like it was in danger of snapping.

As soon as I noticed that, a headache started to form at the base of my skull, and my body hurt.

"I need to go find him," I said, turning around and following my instinct, and the general direction Carl had given me. "I'm new to this whole bond thing, but something tells me Winslow needs me right now."

It was a tiny lie. Something screamed at me that I needed Winslow just then. I needed to hold him in my arms and breathe in his scent. I needed to kiss him and tell him everything would be alright, he hadn't ruined my life, and things were about to get amazing for both of us.

Chapter Nineteen

Winslow

I got antsier and antsier as I watched Mr. Crane walk up the street toward me. My hands started shaking a bit too, but I gripped the two omega pamphlets tightly to stop it, squashing them in the process. I couldn't really go through with it, could I?

I could if I wanted Ty to be happy. It wasn't like I would be doing it for me, and I definitely wouldn't get off on the whole thing. In fact, the idea of letting Mr. Crane so much as shake my hand made me want to puke.

But if I wanted to make things right for Ty and undo all the damage I'd done, I didn't have much of a choice.

Right?

Fuck, I was in over my head.

"Waiting for someone?" Mr. Crane asked with a smile that felt slimy as he came to a stop a little too close to me. Definitely too close for an omega he knew belonged to someone else.

I belonged to someone else. I belonged to Ty.

I swallowed, then answered, "Yeah, sort of. I guess."

I wasn't usually so tongue-tied around alphas. I didn't usually have a hard time talking to anyone. But there was something about Mr. Crane.

Or maybe it was something about the thing I was thinking of doing with him.

Mr. Crane stepped even closer, pulling on the top edges of the pamphlets so I was forced to tip them to where he could read the titles.

He hummed. "You've visited the omega clinic just down there, I see," he said, then smiled up at me again. "Confused about a few things, are you?"

I had to do it. I had to do something to take responsibility for everything I'd done.

"Maybe a little," I mumbled.

He lowered his hand from the pamphlets, brushing my skin as he did. His fingers lingered around my wrist, a little too close to my racing pulse.

"Life as an omega can be confusing, if you don't have the right alpha to keep you in line," he said, playing his fingertips around my speeding pulse. "Your Mr. Martin seems nice and all, but I think I know your type."

"You do?"

I doubted it. Seriously. And something about Mr. Crane made me want to run for the hills.

Something else had my feet glued to the sidewalk. It would just be a short, small thing, and then Ty would be free. It would be gross and maybe painful, and I would probably hate myself for the rest of my life, but did that really matter if Ty could be an ESA again and live his dreams?

"Sure, I do," Mr. Crane said.

His smile stayed in place, but he glanced around, looking back over his shoulder especially, then shifted to cup my elbow and walk me toward the narrow alley between the two buildings to my left.

"I was married once, you know," he said, stopping a few feet inside the alley and stepping toward me in a way that forced my back up against one brick wall. "He was good-looking, but dumb. And he didn't know his place. We have two kids together, but he cheated on me and ran off with a puny beta, of all things." He huffed and shook his head.

"I'm...sorry about that?" I squirmed, holding my arms up with the pamphlets between us like a shield.

I'd thought I could do this, but staring into Mr. Crane's dark eyes and breathing in the scent of too much cologne was making me wonder if I actually had it in me.

But I had to. For Ty's sake.

Mr. Crane put one hand on the wall beside my head. His grin was so smug it turned my stomach. Or maybe my stomach was a mess because of what I was contemplating.

"You're not going to run," Mr. Crane said with a grunt. He shook his head. "You're not even going to scream or try to get away from me, are you?"

I opened my mouth, but no sound came out. I'd never been so terrified in my life.

It would all be over soon, and then everything would be the way it was supposed to be.

If you loved someone, you set them free.

Right?

"Omegas are such sluts," Mr. Crane snorted. He leaned in to draw a long breath of my scent right near the pulse point of my neck, then he hummed. "You're all such delicious sluts, though. Heat or no heat, you want it all the time. Believe me, I know."

I started to shake uncontrollably. I wanted to run, but it was too late, and I couldn't.

"That's what alphas in name only, like your Mr. Martin, don't understand," Mr. Crane went on, dragging his nose up my neck to my cheek. "He made me look like a fool in that meeting. He made all of us alphas look like fools by trying to convince us that omegas are useful to society. You lot are only good for one thing, which is ironic, because that's what this entire Bangers & Mash operation is all about. They got one thing right, I'll say that. Omegas exist to be fucked, and that's all."

He grabbed me so fast I dropped the pamphlets. I lost my balance as he pushed me face first against the wall, then reached around to fumble with the fly of my jeans. He got distracted for a moment by rubbing his meaty hand over my cock through the denim. At least I wasn't even a little bit hard.

"Still not trying to run away from me, omega?" he growled against my ear.

I squeezed my eyes shut and pressed my cheek against the cold brick. I was scared and frozen and starting to cry, but I had to do this. It was the only way. I had to save Ty from—

My thought ended abruptly as Mr. Crane unzipped my fly enough to shove his hand down the front of my jeans. My eyes flew open, and I cried out, trying to push him off me.

I thought I could do this for Ty, because I wanted him to be free, to live his life and have his career. I thought I was doing it because I cared about him, because I loved him.

I loved him. So much. Enough to do something monumentally stupid for his sake.

Which meant there was no fucking way I could do this. Not even a little.

"Get off of me!" I shouted, trying to twist and throw my elbows enough to make contact with him and fight him off. "Get off me now!"

"I'll get off, alright," Mr. Crane growled against my ear. "And so will you, you little omega whore. You're all the same."

I struggled as he worked to push my jeans down, but he could only use one hand at a time as long as I struggled. The more I kicked and squirmed, the more he leaned into me, pressing me against the wall. That meant he couldn't get my jeans down, so he switched to trying to undo his own trousers.

"Stop fighting, you little bitch," he growled. "You know you want it. All omegas want it. So stay still and take it."

I had no intention of doing any such thing. But panic was starting to sap my energy. Mr. Crane was just naturally stronger than me anyhow. I wouldn't be able to fight him off for long.

There was only one thing I could think to do besides shouting for help, which I was damn well going to do until my throat ripped.

"Stop!" I shouted. "Help me, help!"

At the same time, I let go of the inner resistance I had clamped around my bond with Ty from the moment I left the office building. I didn't know what I was doing or if it would work, but I imagined turning a faucet on all the way and letting the water gush out.

It was the only thing I could think to do, because I needed Ty. I needed my alpha.

Ty

I KNEW I WAS GETTING CLOSER TO WINSLOW, BUT the pain in my head and my body were getting worse instead of better. That wasn't the way I thought bonds were supposed to work, but if that morning had taught me anything, it was that I didn't actually know shit about being bonded.

"I don't think he would have gone far," Carl said as he walked behind me, taking two steps for every one of mine. I didn't know why he'd followed when he was obviously having such a good time building houses, but I was oddly okay with him tagging along on this mission. "Winslow isn't the sort to wander off. That's more of my department. I once walked all the way to—hey, isn't that Mr. Sanchez and Mrs. Cross in there?"

Carl stopped by the front of a quaint café half a block up the street from the office building. He broke into a smile and waved into the café.

I started to turn toward him, but in a flash, it was like my head split open and my heart exploded. My bond with Winslow went from being weak and confusing to a full-blown hurricane. The sensation was so overpowering that it nearly brought me to my knees.

Worse than the widening of the bond itself, the abject terror that came through from Winslow was so ferocious I nearly vomited. My omega was in trouble. Horrific trouble.

"Winslow!" I shouted, charging up the street at full speed.

"Ty? What's going on?" I vaguely heard Carl ask behind me.

I immediately tuned him out. Winslow was nearby, I could feel it now. More than that, I could hear him. I could hear him calling for help. And not just in my head and heart.

I raced past what looked like an omega services clinic just as a man with a baby opened the door. I came within inches of smashing into him, only dodging at the very last second.

"Is someone in trouble?" another voice from inside the clinic asked.

I ignored them, racing on to the street corner.

"Help! Stop! Get off me!"

I heard Winslow's voice and skidded to a halt just past a narrow alley, then backtracked so fast I strained my neck. I didn't care about my own health and wellbeing right then, though, only Winslow.

I saw him immediately, shoved up against the wall of one of the buildings, Crane right behind him. My vision tunneled with rage at the way Crane was manhandling my omega. I caught just a hint of pink as the bastard tried to take his cock out.

I surged forward, fully intending to rip the man's dick right off.

Crane saw me a half-second too late and reeled back, shouting. He wasted time stuffing his dick back in his trousers instead of running, like he should have, which gave me more than enough time to storm toward him and throw a punch. That punch landed square across his jaw, and if the alley hadn't been so narrow, he would have dropped instead of slamming into the opposite wall from Winslow and gripping it for support.

I would have gone at him again, probably pummeling him into a greasy puddle, if Winslow hadn't gasped, "Ty!" and thrown himself at me.

Everything else stopped as I crushed Winslow into my arms. The primal urge to protect and shelter my omega overrode even my need to punish the man who had tried to hurt him. My anger and thirst for revenge dampened and were overtaken by pure relief and throbbing love.

I picked Winslow up without even thinking about it, and even though I knew it probably hurt his pride on some level, he wrapped his arms around my neck and his legs around my waist and sobbed against my shoulder. His whole body shook as I carried him out of the shadows of the alley and into the sunshine of the street.

"Shh, shh, it's okay, baby, you're going to be okay," I

murmured to him, not unlike the way I'd calmed him that first day, when I'd found him insensible with heat. I stroked his hair and pressed my lips against his head. "I've got you. You're going to be okay."

"Oh my God, what happened?" Carl shouted, skidding to a halt beside us. "Winslow, are you okay?"

I was only peripherally aware of Sanchez, Cross, and several of the city councilmen racing up the street behind Carl. Their eyes were all wide with shock, and when Crane stumbled out of the alley a moment later, dabbing his split lip with the back of his suit jacket sleeve, most of them gasped.

"What's going on here?" one of the councilmen demanded. "Roger?"

"Martin attacked me," Crane spat. He edged his way around me and Winslow, heading to his colleagues, as though they would protect him. I was worried that they actually would.

I was more worried that I was about to watch the entire B&M branch deal blow up in my face.

"Attacked you?" Sanchez asked, darting a glance between me and Crane.

"He tried to...harm my omega," I growled. If ever there was a time to let my alpha loose, it was now. I didn't care what it did to the B&M deal. Work was work, and even though I loved it, I loved Winslow more. Winslow was my life.

"That scrawny omega wanted it," Crane argued, red-faced and sweating. "Omegas are all whores anyhow."

"I beg your pardon?" Cross said, turning to Crane with a murderous look.

Crane had evidently forgotten who was standing around him. Cross wasn't the only one who looked aghast at his statement, nor was Sanchez—though he looked like he would defend his wife the same way I would defend Winslow—to the death. Most of the other councilmen looked astounded as well, and the ones who didn't kept their gazes averted and moved subtly away from Crane, as though he would taint them by association.

"He's just an omega," Crane said, trying a different tactic and appealing to the others as though it were no big deal.

"You've assaulted a man," Sanchez snapped. "You've attacked the omega of an incredibly important business partner. I wouldn't be surprised if Norwalk lost the entire deal because you couldn't keep it in your pants." He nodded to Crane's trousers.

Bizarrely, Crane's fly was mostly undone, and even though he'd tucked himself away, a hairy bit of pink was still showing through the open material.

One of the councilmen made a disgusted sound and turned away. I, on the other hand, had to work hard not to grin in vicious satisfaction. Crane was going to have a hell of a time explaining that one away. And it meant the near-crime had witnesses too.

Crane seemed to catch the predicament he was in. He cleared his throat and did up his fly the rest of the way. "I don't see that it matters whether Norwalk ends up with one of these ridiculous heat support freak shows anyhow," he said. "You know I've been against it from the start, and I have been telling Mayor Kenzie—"

He stopped as the sound of police sirens wailed just around the corner.

"You were saying?" Sanchez asked as the first of the cars turned the corner another street up.

"Cool!" Carl called out, looking like he was having the best day of his life. "It's like a real-life cop show or something."

I sent Carl a flat, quelling look. I must have still looked ferocious, because Carl immediately shut up and hunched in on himself.

"Who called the police?" Crane demanded. "And why? Because some cheap omega threw himself at me?"

"You assaulted my omega," I shouted.

Unfortunately, that caused Winslow to flinch and tense in my arms, and to bury his face harder against my shoulder.

"I'm sorry, baby," I said, ignoring everyone else and focusing just on him. "I didn't mean to shout. I didn't mean to make you feel like you had to go away this morning either. I won't do it again."

Winslow whimpered and shook his head against my shoulder, then struggled until I put him down. When he was on his own two feet, he looked up at me. His pink, tear-streaked face nearly broke my heart.

He sniffled and wiped his face with his sleeve before saying, "No, I'm sorry. I...I thought if I broke our bond, then you could go back to your life the way it was and—"

"Shh, baby, it's okay," I said, cutting him off by pulling him into my arms.

I needed him to keep quiet for more reasons than one. I didn't know the laws in Norwalk well enough to know whether anything Winslow said would be held against him. From the sound of things, Crane might be willing to argue Winslow was willing, even though I knew he hadn't been.

"I'm really sorry," Winslow whispered as I held him close.

"I know, baby, I know," I whispered back.

It didn't matter how chaotic the scene was getting around us—and as soon as the cops pulled up and got out to investigate the situation, Crane turned belligerent—I had Winslow back in my arms, where he belonged. Yeah, we had a mountain of things to sort out. We'd both pretty much fumbled the ball of our new relationship, but we could sort things out, I knew we could.

"I tell you, that omega practically threw himself at me,"

Crane was arguing when I forced my attention to expand beyond Winslow.

"That omega has a name," Cross said, facing off with Crane like a pro. "It's Winslow Grant, and he's the mate of Tybalt Martin, a representative from Bangers & Mash who is in town to develop plans to open a branch here in Norwalk."

She was explaining things to the two beta cops who had gotten out of their cars to assess the situation. What surprised me was when a third cop, a man with more brass on his uniform than either of the betas, stepped forward to stare at Crane with narrowed eyes. He was clearly the sergeant, and he was an omega.

"You again, Crane?" the omega sergeant said, shaking his head impatiently as he joined the other two officers.

Crane sneered at the man. "Sergeant Ross," he huffed, shaking his head.

"Now, why am I not surprised to find you when I've been called to an assault of an omega?" Sergeant Ross asked.

"He has a record," one of the beta officers told me, almost as an aside.

That seemed to come as news to Cross, whose eyes went wide. She turned to one of the other councilmen and said, "You put Crane on this committee when he has a record of assaulting omegas?"

"Unbelievable," Sanchez said, shaking his head in disgust. "As if we don't have enough corruption to deal with at city hall."

"Believe me," one of the other councilmen said, looking at Crane with loathing. "If I'd known anything about this, Crane never would have been chosen." He glanced to me and went on with, "Mr. Martin, I sincerely hope this hasn't damaged our chances of bringing a Bangers & Mash branch to Norwalk."

Still another councilman said, "Clearly, we need institutions like Bangers & Mash, not to mention men like you and your omega, here in Norwalk more than ever."

"I hope you'll consider coming back to the table with us this afternoon to continue on with plans and to discuss ways we can make up for this pitiful display," the first councilman said.

I hugged Winslow closer, feeling good about things despite the turmoil.

"That's all up to Winslow," I said, letting him go so that he could stand by my side and regain some of his pride. "If he feels like Norwalk would be a safe place for him to live, then I'm all for proceeding."

Chapter Twenty

Winslow

Ty's statement took me entirely by surprise.

"Live?" I asked, blinking away the last remnants of my tears. I was so embarrassed to have cried and clung to Ty like a baby monkey in front of so many important people, but that hardly seemed important at the moment.

The weird thing was, I wasn't the only one who looked excited at the statement.

"So your call with your bosses went well?" Mrs. Cross asked, lighting up at the thought.

Ty sent her a polite smile, but I could feel that he was only thinking of me in that moment.

"It went very well," he said, glancing from me to Mrs. Cross and Mr. Sanchez, and several of the councilmen who weren't helping the police deal with Mr. Crane. "Sal is eager to have everything move forward with the branch, and he wants me to head it up and move here to run it."

"That's great news," Mr. Sanchez said, actually breaking into a smile.

I wanted to smile, but I was confused. "Don't they want someone to run this branch who can be an ESA themselves?" I asked, knowing Ty would hear my unspoken question about what that meant for the two of us. It might have been massively stupid for me to even entertain the idea of breaking our bond, but it just occurred to me that Ty could break it the same way, and all in the name of his career.

I knew he could tell what I was thinking as soon as the question was out of my mouth. He pulled me into his arms for probably the most reassuring hug and kiss I'd ever gotten. It was his answer even before he said, "They want me here even though I'm not an ESA anymore and never will be again."

There was way more to that answer than anyone else would know. I hugged him back, letting out a deep breath. Maybe we'd gotten off to a rocky start, but things were going to be okay. Ty made that known with the way he embraced me, the way he touched my face when I finally stepped back, a little too aware that we were being watched, and through the unconditional acceptance I could feel through the bond.

We were going to be okay.

Although I still had a hell of a lot of apologizing to do for being stupid about Mr. Crane.

"Ty, I'm sorry—"

"And guess what?" Carl interrupted, bounding up to us, his face full of excitement. "I'm moving to Norwalk with you."

My mouth hung open from my apology, and I turned to my brother, bristling with frustration. Our audience of councilmen had pretty much disbanded as most of them had gone into the café, and Mr. Sanchez had peeled off to deal with the police as they prepared to take Mr. Crane away. One of them lingered on the corner of the scene, like he wanted to talk to me and Ty, probably to get a statement, but I had to deal with Carl first.

"Carl," I said, as firmly as I'd ever spoken to him, taking a step toward him. "You're my brother and I love you, but you need to stop relying on me for everything. I'm with Ty now, and if you want to move to Norwalk too, that's fine, but I want to build a real, strong relationship with my alpha, and eventually, I want us to have a family. Which means you can't interrupt whenever I'm trying to have a moment with Ty."

Carl gaped at me, somewhere between shocked that I would speak to that way, and maybe a little hurt, and amused for some reason.

His shocked look dropped, and he said, "I was just going to tell you that I want to move to Norwalk too, because I was offered a job working for the construction company building all those houses," he said. The way he spoke made him sound more grown-up than I'd ever heard Carl sound.

"Oh," I said, lowering my head a bit and rubbing the back of my neck. "That's great. Shit, Carl, I'm sorry I snapped at you."

"Hey, I get it," Carl said, still sounding grown-up. "I haven't been the easiest to deal with since Mom died. And that probably isn't going to change too much." He grinned and looked sheepish. "Something has just clicked for me today while working on the houses. I don't know what it is." He shrugged. "Maybe it has something to do with being able to climb around while working instead of being stuck in a store somewhere. Or maybe it's the promise of working with a nail gun."

I laughed, especially when I felt a deep wave of wariness through the bond.

"Or maybe it's the fact that I know you're taken care of, so I don't have to worry about getting interested in something that might take me away from you and leave you alone," Carl went on, emotion suddenly flooding his expression.

I blinked. "Is that what you've been concerned about all this time?" I asked. "Why you haven't done more things or looked for better work?"

"You're my little brother," Carl said with a shrug. "We're all that the two of us have left in the world."

It was astoundingly sweet of him, and it put everything from the last few years into perspective. I wouldn't have chosen to show my love for my brother by getting fired over and over so I could spend time with him, but Carl had a unique way of thinking.

"I knew you would like the construction project," Mrs. Cross said, stepping into the conversation. "Something just told me it would be a good fit."

"So you arranged this whole thing," Ty said like he was connecting the dots. He put his hand on the small of my back when I stepped back to him.

Mrs. Cross smiled modestly. "I had a hunch the moment I met you all," she explained. "And I've gotten to where I am in this world by knowing when to put the right people together at the right time. I'd like to continue to use that as we build this alliance between Bangers & Mash and the city of Norwalk."

I smiled. I liked Mrs. Cross. She was not your typical omega at all. I hoped I would get to know her better, and maybe learn a thing or two from her about, well, everything.

"Sorry to interrupt," the police officer who had been standing by stepped in. "Mr. Grant, we just need to get a statement from you."

The next fifteen minutes or so were spent with me explaining what had happened with Mr. Crane to the police. It was surreal to tell the quick story of my stupidity in not running or screaming when I could. I could sense that Ty was nervous about everything I said to the police, and I couldn't blame him—half because rich alphas like Mr. Crane tended to get away with crimes against omegas, and half because I really had been monumentally stupid.

Once that was taken care of, we all went into the café for lunch—except Carl, who wanted to get back to building houses. It was surreal to sit down with Mrs. Cross and Mr. Sanchez and the city councilmen and to try to proceed as though nothing unusual had happened. Everyone was on edge, the councilmen were ridiculous with their apologies, and I felt awkward the whole time.

But not as awkward as I could have felt. After lunch, when everyone returned to the office for more meetings, I went with them. I went with Ty really, because more than ever, I didn't want to be apart from him. Not just because of the bond or some external feeling like the two of us were linked and I needed to stay near him, but because I suddenly had a sense that I was a part of something, a part of Ty's life instead of something that had swept in and ruined it.

"I don't know what Mr. Martin or Bangers & Mash has in mind for your participation in this project," Mr. Sanchez said to me toward the end of the afternoon, as everything was starting to wrap up, "but my wife and I would definitely like to involve you in our business in some way."

I blinked, glanced to Ty for a second, then looked back to where Mr. Sanchez and Mrs. Cross were sitting at the end of the conference table, smiling at me. "Me?" I asked.

"Yes, you," Mrs. Cross said, almost laughing.

"But I've never been to college. I'm only twenty. I don't have a lot of experience with real jobs," I argued.

Ty took my hand under the table, and it felt like he gave me a jolt of his confidence.

"That's what training programs are for," Mrs. Cross said happily. "I'm sure between all of us, we can get you into exactly the right program to train for a career that's perfect for your skills."

I wanted to argue that I didn't have any skills, but something stopped me. I was just starting out. I was just at the beginning. People had to start somewhere. No one was born at the top of their game. I could do this. Mrs. Cross had faith in me, and way more importantly, Ty had faith in me too.

Maybe I hadn't ruined Ty's career. Maybe I had inadvertently stumbled into a real career of my own.

I told Ty as much later that night, as we were getting ready for bed after a long day of meeting and schmoozing over supper.

"Of course this is the beginning of something," Ty said. We were still in the bathroom, brushing our teeth and washing our faces, but he swept me into his arms just as I put my toothbrush down. "I think you will do brilliantly at whatever you decide to take on."

His confidence in me was amazing. I got all emotional, blinking and turning my face to the side, trying to fight off tears. I hoped it was the lingering effects of heat still and not me turning into a typical, emotional omega.

"I was your age when I started with Bangers & Mash," Ty went on. He rested a hand on the side of my face and turned it so I was looking at him again. He reflected what I'd been thinking all day by saying, "Everyone has to start somewhere."

"Thanks, Ty," I said, relaxing in his arms and letting my shoulders drop a little. "No one has ever had that kind of confidence in me."

He smiled broadly at me. "You're my omega. I'll always support you, no matter what you want to do with your life. You want a career? I'll help you in every way I can. You want a family?" His grin turned wicked. "I will definitely help with that. And if you want both?"

He answered with a mischievous flicker of one eyebrow,

then leaned in to slant his mouth over mine in a perfect, hot kiss. All I wanted to do was fall into that kiss and get lost forever. I loved Ty so much. I didn't know how it happened, and while people might have questioned me falling for someone I'd only known for a week, I didn't care. Love wasn't logical, and there was no point in waiting or second-guessing when you found the person you knew beyond a shadow of a doubt you were meant to be with.

That was when a huge wave of guilt crashed into me.

I pulled out of Ty's arms and sent him a deeply embarrassed look.

"I'm so, so sorry Ty," I mumbled.

"Here we go with the apologies again," Ty said, teasing me. He pulled me back into his arms, swept a hand over my face, and tilted it up to him. He kissed my lips softly, then said, "I told you, you didn't ruin my career or my life. I was shortsighted to think that nothing would change, that I wouldn't be able to adapt and take another path along the same journey. And honestly, I know, deep in my soul, that everything is going to be so much better with you by my side."

I smiled, but his beautiful words only made me have to fight harder not to cry.

"That's not what I'm sorry for this time," I said, my voice cracking a little. I lowered my head and said, "I'm sorry I let Mr. Crane talk to me like that, sorry I let him get that close to me."

"You have nothing to be sorry for," Ty said in an angry voice. I knew his anger was for Mr. Crane, but I still felt awful as he took my hand and led me into the bedroom, sitting on the bed with me. "That man was a predatory ass. There is nothing you could have done that would make you even a little bit guilty of what he tried to pull with you."

My insides squirmed as I worked up my nerve to confess.

"I thought that I could break our bond and set you free," I

blurted the words before I could chicken out. "I'd been thinking about it, and then Mr. Crane came along, and for a split second, but only a split second, I thought that might be the solution to our problems."

I could feel Ty's reaction. He was alarmed and a little bit angry, but I could tell again that anger wasn't directed at me.

More than that, he shifted the way he sat on the bed so he could pull me fully into his embrace. I straddled his lap, which brought us into such close contact that a whole different set of emotions and needs began to fire through me.

"I should be the one to apologize," Ty said, stroking my hair, my neck, and down my arms.

"You weren't an idiot, like I was," I said.

"Yeah, actually, I think I was," Ty said, surprising me. He cradled my face in those big hands of his and said, "I was an idiot for making you feel, even for one moment, like you were anything but a blessing to me. I should have been so much clearer with you about how much I care about you. I love you, Winslow."

Even another alpha would have let loose with the tears at that statement. I sobbed a little before hiccupping to stop myself and said, "But we barely know each other. You didn't ask for me to come into your life. I was a mistake."

"You could never be a mistake," Ty said, underlining the statement with a kiss. "I don't care if we've known each other a week or our whole lives. You are a part of me, Winslow Grant, whether either of us expected it or not."

"I wasn't even who you were supposed to meet up with that day," I argued, though the words were mostly just my head dumping out the last of its thoughts so that my heart could take over.

"You might have been the wrong omega for that call," Ty said, smiling as he brushed my tears away with his thumbs, "but you are absolutely the right person for me to spend the rest of my life with. I'm sorry that I ever made you doubt that."

My heart throbbed in my chest, and I smiled at Ty. "We're going to get better at this whole relationship thing, right?" I asked, sniffling.

Ty laughed. "God, I hope so. We couldn't get much worse."

"Not the best of starts," I agreed, managing to laugh through my tears. "But I love you too," I said, pouring everything I had into those simple words. "It doesn't really make sense, but I'm not going to worry about that. I love you, I know it, and nothing is going to change that. I wouldn't want anything to change it. You're my family and my future, Ty."

He made a hot, growling sound, then pulled me against him for a kiss that was clearly the beginning of much, much more.

My body responded to him readily, aching and heating, but I put my hands on his chest and pushed away for a moment.

"I do want babies with you," I told him quickly, before lust got the better of me. "Lots of them. But I want to try to have a career first, and even once we have them."

"Anything you want, baby," Ty purred, then tipped me back to lie under him.

There was probably more to talk about, but it could wait. All I cared about right then was tugging at the t-shirt I'd put on for bed, then wriggling out of it and my pajama bottoms as Ty slipped off his boxers. I made a note to stop sleeping in pajamas at all, but that and every other thought was drowned out as Ty bent down to kiss me into oblivion.

It felt so right, like Ty and I belonged together, like we were two pieces of a puzzle that had clicked into place. Ty left my mouth to kiss his way down my neck and chest to use his tongue to play with one of my nipples. My cock loved that and lay hard and demanding against my belly. I'd never wanted to be fucked as badly as I did right then, with Ty, with my alpha.

"You're so beautiful, baby," Ty said, his voice vibrating through me, as he kissed his way lower still. "Even when you're not in heat, I can't resist you. I want all of you, I want to devour you."

Everything he said was so sexy that I could barely catch my breath. My cock was already leaking, and my balls were tight, even before he reached between my legs to fondle them. I groaned with pleasure and rolled my hips up to him, then let out a cry as he stroked his hand up my cock. If I had any temptation to be jealous or wary of his experience as an ESA, that flew out the window as he shifted lower so he could close his hot, wet mouth around the tip of my cock to suck and lick it. He might have had hundreds of omegas in a professional capacity before, but he was all mine now, and it was deeply personal.

I was putty in his hands as he drew me all the way to the back of his throat, then sucked as he pulled back again. The sensations he sparked in me were so, so good, and even though it was embarrassingly quick, when he repeated the swallowing then sucking sequence, I came hard with an obscene cry.

Ty hummed and laughed a little as he swallowed everything I gave him—which felt like a lot for an omega, though it was probably nothing to him. "I love how freely you give it to me," he panted once I was done and lying in what felt like a puddle of my own slick. And I wasn't even in heat.

I was just about to say something that I hoped would be sexy in reply, but he grabbed hold of me and flipped me to my stomach. He pushed my legs wide apart with enough roughness to leave me catching my breath, then crawled over me, leaning down until I could feel the tickle of his chest hair against my back.

"Now I'm going to give something to you," he purred against my ear with just enough menace to leave me shivering.

I imagined him fucking me hard and deep and making me scream as he took me. The flash of fantasy was unbelievably hot, and it had me wriggling my hips and practically presenting my hole to him to be filled.

Instead of going straight for it, Ty landed a feather-light kiss on the back of my neck. He followed that with another and another and another, making a lazy trail of kisses down my spine. I was still trapped, spread, and helpless beneath him, but there wasn't any other place I would rather have been.

I felt drunk with pleasure by the time his trail of kisses reached the small of my back, then the top of my ass.

"You smell so good," Ty growled, grabbing the top of my thighs with his big hands and pushing my legs apart farther to open me up all the way to him. "That dripping hole is the hottest thing I've ever seen."

I twitched at those words, and Ty made a wolfish sound of approval as my hole leaked ridiculously for him. I didn't know what he was used to, and I had pretty much zero experience myself, but I had the feeling all of my slutty, omega reactions were fueling his hottest fantasies.

"Baby," he purred, drawing his fingers across my opening hole and the slick that pooled there as I arched my back. I didn't know if he was talking about me or what he wanted to spend a lot of time and effort putting into me.

A moment later, it didn't matter. He lowered himself, and his mouth was over my hole like he wanted to fuse it there. I let out a raunchy moan as he thrust his tongue into me over and over, sending my senses reeling. I didn't know if I was supposed to be this sensitive and horny when I wasn't even in heat or if the bond had something to do with it, but I definitely wasn't complaining.

My cock twitched to life again as Ty licked and swept his

tongue around my hole, lapping up the slick that ran from me like someone had left the faucet on. It was so good that I jerked against him, my body trying to impale itself on his tongue, wanting even more than that.

I said a quick prayer of thanks to whoever had designed omegas to have multiple orgasms as my body tensed and another one hit me. It was a doozy too.

"Fuck, Winslow," Ty growled, watching as my body trembled and contracted. He had an up-close view for the whole thing, and as my groin tightened, he buried his face against my ass.

That wasn't enough for him, apparently. "I want you," he said in deep, broken tones, like he'd meant to say more and make it poetic, but nature wouldn't let him.

Seconds later, he grabbed my hips hard enough to bruise and thrust boldly into me. I cried out with how good it felt to be taken that way. Fuck being a strong, confident omega. I just wanted my alpha to stuff me and make me cry with pleasure and come for a third time. It felt too good just to be Ty's fuck hole.

Or maybe that was strength on my part. I wanted it, so I claimed it. I all but howled with pleasure as he stuffed me, grunting and thrusting and firing every nerve in my body. And when he curled over me, fucking harder, then came with a roar, I lost it and spilled everything I had for the third time.

It was wild, primal, and so, so good, and for a while after, neither of us could move. I loved the weight of Ty's body over mine and the feel of him still inside of me, even though it wasn't heat and he couldn't knot me. It was the next best thing.

"This," I said as soon as I was able to speak through my panting. "This is the best thing I've every felt in my life."

Ty started to laugh as his lust gave way to far tenderer emotions. He pulled out of me—which I didn't like—and rolled us so that we could lie tangled up together, face-to-face —which I definitely did like.

"I love you, Winslow," he said, but with far deeper emotion than before. "I don't know what I did before you."

"I love you too, Ty," I panted, snuggling into him. "And before doesn't matter. We're together now, and our life together is going to be awesome."

I HOPE YOU'VE ENJOYED TY AND WINSLOW'S STORY! These two were so much fun to write! And there's more of *Bangers & Mash* to come!

REMEMBER JUSTIN, ONE OF THE NEW ESAs IN THE training class in *How to Train Your Alpha*? Well, it's time for his very first ESA call ever! And, of course, things don't go to plan. Find out just what happens in *New Alpha on the Block*.

IF YOU ENJOYED THIS BOOK AND WOULD LIKE TO hear more from me—as MM Farmer or my other identities, Merry Farmer (Historical Romance and more) or Em Farmer (Contemporary Romance) please sign up for my newsletter! When you sign up, you'll get your choice of a free, full-length novella. One choice is *A Passionate Deception*. It is an MF romance, but it has a strong MM secondary character, who gets his own book in my May Flowers series. Part of my West Meets East series, *A Passionate Deception* can be read as a stand-alone. Your other choice is *Rendezvous in Paris*. It is an MM Victorian story that is part of my *Tales from the Grand Tour* series, but can also be read as a standalone. Pick up your free copy today by signing up to receive my newsletter (which I only send out when I have a new release)!

Sign up here: http://eepurl.com/cbaVMH

Are you on social media? I am! Come and join the fun on Facebook: http://www.facebook.com/merryfarmerreaders

I'm also a huge fan of Instagram and post lots of original content there: https://www.instagram.com/merryfarmer/

And, oh gosh, I signed up for TikTok too! They never should have let me on there, but if you want to watch me embarrassing myself in videos, you can follow me here: https://www.tiktok.com/@merryfarmer

About the Author

I hope you have enjoyed *The Wrong Omega*. If you'd like to be the first to learn about when new books in the series come out and more, please sign up for my newsletter here: http://eepurl.com/cbaVMH And remember, Read it, Review it, Share it! For a complete list of works by Merry Farmer with links, please visit http://wp.me/P5ttjb-14F.

USA Today Bestselling author Merry Farmer—who writes Omegaverse as MM Farmer—is an award-winning novelist who lives in suburban Philadelphia with her cats, Justine and Peter. She has been writing since she was ten years old and realized one day that she didn't have to wait for the teacher to assign a creative writing project to write something. It was the best day of her life. She then went on to earn not one but two degrees in History so that she would always have something to write about. Her books have reached the Top 100 at Amazon, iBooks, and Barnes & Noble, and have been named finalists in the prestigious RONE and Rom Com Reader's Crown awards.

Acknowledgments

I owe a huge debt of gratitude to my awesome beta-readers, Erica Montrose and Jolene Stewart, for their suggestions and advice. And double thanks to Julie Tague, for being a truly excellent editor and to Cindy Jackson for being an awesome assistant!

Click here for a complete list of other works by Merry Farmer.